The Seven Disclosures of a Trans Woman

by

Eva Odland

All text copyright © Eva Odland 2013

Published by Bradly A. Odland

1st Print Edition November, 2013

ISBN-13: 978-1492773467

This is a work of fiction. Any resemblance of persons alive or dead is purely coincidental.

Cover photo Dimitrii | © Dreamstime Stock Photos & Stock Free Images

One

I sat on one of the benches in the front of the small cafe waiting for her. She said 11:30 but me being me I wanted to be early, so I was sure to be waiting. I looked at my watch, 11:10. Maybe I was too eager. I do this all the time, some sort of OCD thing maybe—arrive early then sit, waiting. I get the best seat but whatever, it's a lovely day and this spot has some prime people watching.

I met Kylie recently. I'm not sure why I am on a third date, if you could call it a date. Seemed more like were just really friendly people who liked to share a meal once in a while. At least that is what we seem to be doing. For some reason I hadn't made any romantic intentions clear to her, even after two really fun meetings. I saw her on the bus that day and took the chance and asked her to meet for cocktails after work. We had a few drinks and some appetizers. We talked and laughed as any new relationship just starting would, but there is something about her I couldn't put my finger on. Something that made me feel oddly uneasy. But still, she is so pretty, unusually pretty, almost shocking even. I didn't get why she was not with anyone and then to say yes to me. I am mean I'm not a dork or anything like that but I could stand to lose a few pounds, maybe have some nicer clothes. What was I looking for? I was between gigs so to speak and I was on contract here in town. Not permanent so what do I care? When this contract is up I might move on down the road.

Either way I'm just looking for excitement, and so far she has really excited me. She is tall. I mean not like WNBA tall. Which is really cool because I am 6'2" and finding a girl that is only a couple inches shorter than me is a losing proposition. I think I maybe dated two girls near six foot in my life. But we didn't work out and I was young and made some screw ups myself. I have my own issues to deal with. I am a tall guy and I am not height prejudice when it comes to women. Tall or short, wide, curvy or thin if they "have it" that weird thing that I can't figure out what it is, if they have that, I get stuck on them, at least for a while.

Kylie definitely has that thing. She has that strong determined super model like face that scares the shit out most guys. It takes a guy with a ton of confidence to go with a chick a head taller than he is. I, fortunately have not suffered much from being shorter than women I date. Unless you count guys. Well, I would be lying to myself if I said 'date'. I dabbled some.

Sometimes for some reason a guy catches my eye or maybe he catches me staring and well. Lets just say, I've played on the other side of the fence before. I don't consider myself gay or bisexual but I suppose most could argue that claim. Maybe I haven't accepted the label. I just know for some reason my attraction doesn't always constrain me specifically to women and I just go with it, to a fault I guess. Explains why at 34 I am still single and essentially a well-to-do homeless man, an IT vagabond traveling from place to place. Oh, I have an apartment, but I am never there. I'm use to staying a few months maybe a year then moving on. Who do I have to answer to? Just the people signing my paychecks and most of the time it is myself. So I guess from time to time, I indulge myself in some man love, it doesn't make me any less a man.

So why if I like being with another man would I be looking for women? I like them too.

I find people attractive, not just some gender. I know a lot of people won't understand that and that is why I am who I am. I don't have a lot of friends, gay or straight. Gay men don't trust me because I am attracted to women but they sure as hell like to have sex with me. Women, well it takes a unique woman to open the door for me to tell my story. Something I still haven't really done yet. Maybe Kylie is the one, who knows. But regardless I have been missing female companionship of late. I haven't been on many dates with women in the past couple years. In fact I have been on many at all, unless you count Grindr hookups.

I am missing too much. No emotional attachment, no commitment. Love. I guess I found I'm not really able to fall in love with a guy. Confused? Yeah pretty much.

There she is walking down the street. I can see her. Damn she is beautiful. I can't help but notice my palms are feeling flushed and I might even be nervous. That just cracks me up that I can be nervous. But she does that every time I see her.

Why am I so nervous?

I found out.

***

I couldn't understand, I mean it was pretty outrageous when she first told me. There we were in the cafe, middle of lunch. I didn't really believe her at first but after she just sat there, staring at me, I had no other reason to believe otherwise.

"Steven, I am transgender."

No lead up or explanation, we were sitting in the window at the place where we had met a week prior, we were talking about recent books and she mentioned she was reading a novel whose main character was transgender. I asked her why would you want to read about trannies. I guess I just blurted it out.

She just stared at me and sipped her coffee, put it back on the table and carefully folded her hands. She leaned forward and with a very serious look on her face, said it.

Steven, I am transgender.

What does that mean? As her words reverberated in my head I kept asking myself, 'What does it mean?' Mostly, what does it mean about me?

Steven I am transgender.

Here I am just a dude looking for someone to share some aspect of my shell of a life I live, was I so desperate for companionship that I didn't see this? How could I? Look at her. She is beautiful. How could I not be attracted to her? Sitting across from her at his tiny table in a nondescript coffee house I just went a little numb, then cold. But why? What is the problem? She looks like a woman. She talks like a woman. She moves like a woman. She is a woman.

Steven I am transgender.

There it is bouncing across my head. I can feel myself keeping my face purposely still. But my heart is leaping up in my throat and my mouth went dry.

Did you hear what I said?

I wasn't expecting that. 'Transgender?' Is it so wrong? What is wrong with that? I searched my memory and my experiences. There were some trans women in my past, friends of friends, a drag queen or two in some anonymous gay bar in some city. Then there were the odd effeminate men in women's clothes that sometimes appeared at backyard parties or clubs. Someone would whisper suddenly and nod. "Look Angie's friend Naomi is here. See? The girl just getting a drink, she's a man." I thought about a party last year, it was one of those moments that a person sticks in your mind. I saw the trans woman and I couldn't stop watching her. Not creepy watching just I kept noticing her as the party ensued.

I would look casually. Like I was just scanning the room I saw men and women. I didn't see *transgender*. I didn't get that some of those petty women would insist on saying 'he is a man'. I didn't see a man. I saw tits, hips, nice legs, pretty hair and a soft face. There were no big muscles or beards. Yeah maybe the hands were a little mannish but I simply don't think these women are men. They are women.

Usually as the evening wore on I would find myself scanning the crowd more and more trying to see what she was doing. I would find her sitting on the edge of a sofa sipping a drink alone. She kept returning to the same place it was a like a safe black hole in the room, like one of the tables at a restaurant that servers seem to ignore. I thought I would change that so I walked over and to say Hi.

We exchanged greetings and a little small talk. We noticed a group women talking in the corner while glaring at me and I say I better get back to my friends. Looking over my shoulder she saw them all staring at us and told me I had better or they might attack and kill us with fire. I laughed and said it was nice meeting her. She smiled and reciprocated and then thanked me. I asked what for and she said for using *"her"* and smiled.

Such a simple thing. Saying, *her.* It just fell out of my mouth but apparently it meant a lot. As I walked back to the other side of the room. I thought about how the other women called her a man, I think I understood why she thanked me. I turned and she was chatting with another person standing near her. I saw her still smiling and that tentative frightened look was missing.

That was the extent of my experience with a trans person. Small talk at a party or tipping the drag queen with the breasts at a bar after work with some other programmers. Hanging out and doing shots. The girl at the party was different. The drag queens don't seem anything like her but I noticed some of the performers appeared to be transgender despite the stage persona. I recall hearing one saying something about when she *"started the change"*, but this right now. This is new. This is not a stranger or some fun party people at a club. This is Kylie and she is my date. I like her and want to be with her. And yet her words continue to echo in my head.

Steven I am transgender.

Shocker. Looking back, I stopped talking to Naomi two years ago at that party because I was afraid of what others would think of me. Here was this interesting beautiful girl, alone at a party and I stopped talking to her because of my fear, and they say I am man. It was pretty weak really. I could have had some sort of interesting relationship, a highlight in my mostly dull existence.

Steven. Did you hear me? Steven?

STEVEN.

The last 'Steven' snapped me out of my synaptic storm. To cover, I took a long slow sip of coffee and stared at her over my cup. Her face looked a little flush and her eyes narrowed with the beginnings of anger. I better speak soon.

"That's cool," I said like I've heard a thousand other trans women tell me.

She scrunched up her face and looked at me with this sort of incredulous look. Then finally she shook her head and said, "You are so full of shit."

"I am?"

She got me.

"I am. I totally am. I am freaking out a little right now. You *are* kidding me, right?" I said.

"No Steven I am not. I needed to tell you sooner or later, that is why we are here."

Damn, is this some kind of gag?

"No really, did one of my friends call you or something and put you up to this?"

"No. No one called me. I am telling you something important about myself. If we are going to see each other more, then I needed to let you know."

"So you chose now, while we were having coffee? No wait. First I don't believe you look me in the eye and tell you are serious."

She smiled and leaned in closer and looked me dead in the eyes with hers. I took stock, perfect eye makeup blended well with her face, maybe too perfect, soft cheekbones, and full lips, pert nose and rounded chin, no facial hair, no stubble. Nothing. There is no 'dude' here.

"You are seriously transgender?"

"I am serious." She said blankly.

"You are trans? And what about—"

"I am trans and it is okay to ask me about that," she said slamming the door shut on any comment I had brewing in my brain stem so I paused. Rephrased.

"So you were a dude and now, obviously you aren't?"

"Technically I never really was a 'dude' but, yes I for all purposes in society I am female."

"I don't get it, technically? I mean you were born with, a penis right? And got the M on your birth certificate?"

"Okay yes, I was born and treated like a boy for most of my childhood. Until I was around 14 or so."

"So you are trans like, with all that going on down there, surgery and such, you had surgery?" I said waving my hands around my crotch.

She looked at me, her eyes narrowed and I saw those little muscles on the sides of jaw flex. I pissed her off.

"No I have not had surgery, I have a penis."

I looked at this beautiful girl that I have been totally enamored with just tell me she has a penis. It sort of blows your mind a bit when a chick tells you she has a penis. It really isn't something you just casually run across in conversation.

"Oh and by the way, right here in my panties, is a dick." Just doesn't happen but hey what the fuck, it is happening now.

I guess I need to think for a change.

"I'm sorry, I shouldn't of asked that. I don't know quite what to say," I said.

"All you have to do is say, 'it's okay' or 'no problem', hell even, 'can I see your penis?'. Anything really, I am use to it all, I'm getting pretty good at it now."

My mind sort of blanked out of a moment or two and I just keep looking at her. *Her.* I guess that is the key here.

Her.

"So, I might need to ask some questions if that is okay."

I stalled as my mind clamored to grasp her statement.

"pretty good at it now"

"What do you mean by pretty good at it? I take it you have done this before?"

"I have, several times, you are number seven."

"Seven, really?— that's something. So you have had this same conversation with others?"

"Not the exact conversation but each time there was a point when I had to disclose my status, as they say."

"Who are 'they'— am I asking too many questions?"

"Therapists. You know the smart people that tell people how to live and No, you can ask questions, I expected you would, else I would not of told you."

She was beginning to become annoyed. I was surprised at myself that I wasn't more shocked or outraged even. But actually I became more intrigued, this whole process of disclosure fascinated me and I wanted to know more. As is the idea of a beautiful woman with a penis sitting in front of me.

"Okay, you are trans, you told me that much. I am pretty open minded person and I can tell you that I am not freaking out, but I guess I deserve to probe a little farther. As you said, if we are going to continue what appears to be a relationship, we do need to talk."

I paused and sat silent for a few seconds and tried to casually take a sip of coffee. I wasn't really sure I was into the idea of having a trans girlfriend but I wasn't finding that indicated I was against it either. Except for the penis thing. She looked at me, at first with a slight scowl on her face and I could see she was just about to give up. Her anxiety level must have been building but she appeared to settle and managed a smile and took a sip of her coffee as well.

"I do understand how difficult this must be. I want you to know, I'm okay for now. Are you okay?"

She let out a long breath and seemed to let go of some tension in her shoulders and the little jaw muscle twitch stopped and her face softened.

"I'm okay. This part is always difficult and I get so sick of doing this over and over again. Sometimes it is breezy easy and other times it is a fucking nightmare."

She looked sad as she was obviously recalling. I pressed on, despite crunching the egg shells we were on.

"So what happened with the other six people you told, that must be difficult and dangerous sometimes. You don't mind me asking, do you?"

She looked puzzled and was about to speak but then she sat back and sipped her coffee again. She put the cup back on the table and nodded slowly as if ending a tiny debate in her mind.

"Actually so far your response has been unique, you didn't try to hit me or get up shouting or walk out, in fact you seem pretty calm, that is good. I haven't had anyone ask me about how it was before, this is different. I'll tell, but I warn you, it is not all pleasant."

Her face drooped slightly and she gazed out the window watching the cars at the stop light and the people at the outside tables. She took another sip of coffee and turned to me again.

"Are you sure you want to hear this?"

"I am."

"The whole story on each with sordid, details?"

"Especially the sordid details, after all wouldn't any other couple want to know about each other after a few dates, more details you know?" he said.

"Okay then,here is a good one to start with..."

Eva Odland

Peter

She saw him watching her as she walked the isles. He kept poking his head around the corners and appearing as she browsed the stacks of books. She was walking into the 'Gender Studies' no so ironically next to 'Women's Studies' and across from 'LGBT' when she spotted him. He sat against the rack pursuing a book, 'Feminism in the Age of Advertising and Mass Consumption'

"Excuse me," he said looking up at Kylie, "I'm hogging up the isle."

She pulled a book off the rack and flipped through the pages as he stood.

"That's okay."

He smiled at her nervously and put the book back on the shelf.

"I've seen you here before, you come in a lot," he said nervously.

Kylie turned her head, acknowledging that he said something and then looked at him with a slightly defensive expression.

"Oh no, don't take that the wrong way. I—I was trying to find some way to talk to you. I'm not really good at this."

"Obviously not," she said.

"No—no I mean, I'm not trying to pick you up, I just wanted to meet you." his words deflated him as they left his mouth and his face turned loose.

"Oh, never mind—" he said as he turned to walk away.

"Wait. It's okay. I have seen you here before too," she said.

He stopped and turned, half smiling half surprised.

"You have? Oh, that's cool,"

He was awfully cute in a nerdish way. She had seen him at the bookstore many times and at other stores on occasions. They had caught each other's eyes a few months ago and after that they seemed to notice each other frequently in the small neighborhood book shop.

Kylie was not used to having this kind of attention, in fact she rather avoided it as much contact as possible. Typically her only interactions during the week were to place an order for food, ask a question or two at a store, or to pay one of the many bills denied by her health insurance.

He looked at his watch and then from side to side, finally at his shoes then he mustered up the courage to ask her, "Would you like to have lunch with me? Across the street is a nice cafe if you want too?"

She smiled and put the book back in the shelf and said, "You move fast. Not even any small talk about feminists in contemporary consumer culture?"

"I figure why do small talk with us both hungry when we could save that for the cafe."

"Makes scense—why not?"

"Oh great. Shall we go now or do you want to talk about feminism and consumerism first?" he said.

She smiled and said, "We can save that for the cafe."

They started to exit the isle together and he stopped and held out his hand.

"Oh my, I almost forgot. I'm Peter, you can call me Pete, if you want, most people do."

"Kylie."

She took his hand, it was col and slightly damp.

They walked to the front of the store, he nodded at the cashier an older woman with bright red hair. She smiled and said, "Thanks for stopping in."

"Thanks."

They walked across the street to the small funky cafe across from the busy bookstore. They walked in and a server waved them to sit anywhere. They picked a booth against the far wall and slid in across from each other. They each pulled their phones out and started checking messages, then set their phones on the table. The server came by with water glasses and filled them with lemon ice water. He explained the lunch special and soup of the day and gave them each a menu.

They looked them over.

"I had the falafals. Very good," he said.

"Yes, they are but I am in the mood for the greatest sandwich ever."

"Really, what's that?"

"Braunschwieger and onions on toasted foccacia," Kylie said.

"Really, yuk. I'll have the roast beef and cheese with a cup of soup."

"Not a liver fan?"

"Yeah no. Uh-uh, but don't let me stop you. That stuff is awful."

"Yes, yes it is offal." she said.

He looked at her with a groan.

"That was bad."

"It was."

The moment passed and they continue to scan the menu in silence. Kylie looked up and found Peter smiling at her.

"What? Is there something on my face?" Kylie said with her face turning a little red.

"No, no. Just looking at you. I'm glad you started coming in to the bookstore. It seems that so few people are coming in as much as they used to."

"I like the place. Good selection and nice people that own it."

"Yeah, Darla and Jim, they are nice, they

are my aunt and uncle."

She smiled and thought that explains why he was always in the store.

"Oh, do you work there?"

"I did when I was in high school. Now I just come here to study and buy books. Sometimes if it gets really busy like at the holidays I help out."

"That is great you have a family business."

He looked a little grim and tore the corner of the napkin and dipped it in his water, rolling it up in the rest of the napkin.

"Yeah, well after my mother passed away, I sort of started hanging out there more."

"Oh, I am sorry."

"Thanks. She passed a few years ago. She was sick for a long time."

"That is terrible, at least she had you with her," she said.

He nodded and saw his face push away the old memories and he started to smile.

"So you from the area? I assume so because I have seen you around the neighborhood."

"Yes, I live a few blocks away, I just moved into town, work you know."

"What do you do?" he asked

"I write and do research. Mostly dry technical articles on engineering and building materials. Pretty geeky stuff. I work from home mostly, which is the best part but it is interesting and pays well."

"That's cool. I'm in insurance, risk management, really dry stuff. I assume you like books."

"Oh yes, I love to read, always have."

"Me too, to a fault, my apartment if littered with books. I can't seem to part with them. Do you use any of those new eReaders?"

"Yes actually here I have this one," she said and pulled a small flat rectangular object from her purse. "I got this a couple years ago. It is pretty addicting. I found I read way more."

"Nice. May I? I haven't got around to one yet, still hooked on real books."

He took the reader from he and touched the button on the front. The screen lit up and showed a book in progress. He read a little then handed it back.

"It looks good, better than the color ones. I would go for these gray models, the text is much cleaner."

She took the reader and put it back in her purse and hung it on her chair. The sat quietly for a few moments and the server brought plates out to them. They proceeded to eat sharing small talk and some thoughts on authors. Kylie felt at ease with him and he was becoming less nervous. His demeanor became more confident and relaxed. Soon he was telling a story about a search for a book that made her laugh.

They locked eyes and she smiled and blushed a little, he smiled back.

"I'm glad you asked me out for lunch. Thank you," she said.

"The pleasure is all mine."

"I don't think I actually have met anyone and went to eat together right away. In fact, to be honest I, haven't really been on a date for quite a while."

"I find that hard to believe. I was really nervous about asking you."

Kylie smiled again. She had attention from

men before but she never allowed it to go beyond simple greetings. She always prevented any further introduction because she was afraid of this situation happening; When she is sitting with a man she was attracted to who knew nothing about who she is. She had always told herself if she was in the situation she would tell him on the first date.

She was lost in thought, her hand was palm down on the table. He reached out and put his hand on hers.

"Are you okay?"

"Oh, sorry, I zoned out a little."

He kept his hand on hers. She tipped her hand up and they interlocked fingers lightly and smiled.

"I like you, I know it sounds corny but I'm really glad I'm here with you," she said.

"Me too."

They paused for a moment and Kylie sighed a little and looked around nervously.

"There is something I need to tell you about me. It is important I get this out before we go any further. I am assuming you will want to ask me out again."

"I was, thinking maybe dinner and a movie Friday would be nice."

She smiled and looked sad at the same time.

"Well then I need to tell you."

She froze a moment and her face belied her strong feelings of fear and anxiety. Inside she was holding back panic that was attempting to take control and have her make some excuse to use the bathroom then fake sick or some other reason to end this now. She could bring herself to leave. Knowing that her life needed to press on, she couldn't wait around for relationships to magically appear. She needed to do this. She wants to tell him, now.

In her mind she already played out that magical moment when the guy just looks at her and says, "Oh that's cool." Total fantasy. She knows what she just did, leaving the store with him to a have lunch was super risky. How was she supposed to learn? How does she move onto the next step, where they will walk and he will reach out to take her hand. How he felt about her strong, oddly large hands? Those answers will only come with trying. She must set herself up for learning how to cope with disclosure. She has played the scenario over and over again and this is going according to her expectations. He seems nice and seems intelligent. Maybe even open minded. Maybe open minded enough to actually be interested in her after he finds out she is plumbed with some of the same parts as he is.

She already traced in her mind the kissing, making out on the sofa after the dinner and a movie. The inevitable reaching for her breast then slowly making her way down to her crotch. She could take charge and give him oral but that just seemed like such a slutty thing to do. If he found out later she was trans during foreplay how bad could that be? It could a be disaster. Her heart sank and she felt her stomach begin to tighten.

There was risk and then there was being stupid. Getting a guy off in some anonymous chillout room at a rave was one thing, but hiding your status giving him head or a hand-job is just too risky. No, she was doing the right thing. Tell him right away, on the first date, before any kissing, before anything sexual.

She took a deep breath and let it out really slow, her anxiety had peaked and she was calming down enough to speak.

"What is it? It can't be that bad. We all have things that we are afraid of."

She looked at him and spoke slowly and clearly, then waited for a response.

"Peter, I am transgender."

Peter sat silent. Slowly his hand slipped away from hers and withdrew under the table. He looked up at her, pain streaked his face mixed with a little anger, but mostly disappointment.

Kylie felt the blood drain from her head and her breath went little short.

"Fuck," Kylie said.

"Oh for fucks sake. Fuck this. You are kidding me? No. No I can't—"

"Can't what?" she said with a hint of anger in her voice.

"Well I can't do this, I'm not like that."

"Like what? What are you not like?" she said now with clear anger in her voice.

"You gotta dick? I'm not a faggot, I don't like men. I like girls. Jesus Christ, yuk! "

His face was going white and bright pink circles formed on his cheeks. His breathing got faster and his eyes began to dart from side to side.

"Do I look like a man?"

"Well no but you, I mean you, don't have a, a—"

"A pussy? Is that what you want? A fucking pussy?" she said loudly that the nearest table looked over.

"Jesus you freak. I almost—fuck," he slammed his fist on the table.

She calmed down, shaking her head, tears were forming in her eyes and she muttered to herself as she fumbled in her purse under the table, *Okay lets go. So what you want to beat me now or after I walk out the door?*

He looked at her but didn't see how vulnerable and saddened she was. He just saw something to strike down. Destroy before it spread.

"No. I can't, not me, I'm no faggot, you can take that tranny bullshit to the gay bar."

"No. Yeah I get it. I'm gone. You are a fucking asshole."

"Hey come on, I'm not the one pretending to be a woman here. You did this on purpose! Tricking me. You tried to trap me!"

Her face went red and he sat up high in his chair and she picked up her water glass and tossed the ice and water into his face.

"Cool it, asshole."

Kylie stood up as Peter was wiping his face off, she grabbed her purse and walked out the door. Tears were streaming down her face as she realized that all went horribly wrong, she should have left earlier, right when those first little red flags started going up. *Stupid!* The thought was screaming at her now. She exited the coffee shop and then started briskly down the sidewalk. She heard footsteps from behind her and Peter yelling at her.

"Fuck you bitch, FREAK!" he yelled and was on her, he grabbed her shoulder.

Kylie stopped and spun on one foot. He stiffened up and his face took a mean look.

"You fucking freak, I liked you! I am gonna fuck your faggot ass up."

Just as he got close and raised his hand, Kylie pulled a small can of pepper spray and squirted it across both his eyes as he raised his fist.

He collapsed screaming on the pavement as he went down Kylie followed him getting the sprayer just inches from his eyes and kept spraying. He went to scream and she filled his mouth and nostril with the stinging spray. He was now violently coughing with foam and mucus running from his face and eyes.

"Fuck YOU, you ignorant fuck," Kylie said.

She turned and calmly walked away and slipped aboard a bus that had stopped at the corner stop. As she walked back and sat down she could see him still writhing on the ground and a few people were stopping wondering what was happening. She quickly sat down and looked forward. Her eyes were wide with panic. She scrambled for her sunglasses in her purse and slipped them on and tried to catch her breath. She felt like someone was choking her and she gasped for more breath and started to panic more. Her head suddenly became fuzzy and light as the bus tipped sideways. The last thing she saw before she passed out was a woman with two grocery bags leaning down looking concerned. Her lips were moving but she wasn't saying anything. There was just the sound of the bus engine and the beach. The sound of waves rushing up the sand. The woman before her faded to black.

When her eyes opened there was a two people in blue shirts with gold emblems of some kind. They were wearing gloves like a doctor. One was shining a flashlight in her eye and she felt one of her eyes being forced open. Her eyebrows furrowed and she tried to speak but it was muffled by something over her mouth and nose. Cool dry air was flowing inside it.

"I think she is coming around," one of the blueshirts said.

"Miss? Can you hear me?"

Kylie heard the heads talking now between blinks she nodded her head.

"Miss you were unconscious. Are you hurt? Do you have any pain?"

Kylie shook her head slightly.

"She was just sitting when I got on the bus and I was watching her she was gasping for breath and then just tipped over," the grocery woman said, "She looked all flustered."

Kylie went to sit up. The world was clear now.

"Miss you should stay down."

"No, I can sit up. I'll be fine. I got dizzy and fainted. I think I hyperventilated. I'm okay."

She sat up and the paramedics watched her.

"Well you should still let us take you to the hospital. You were out for about fifteen minutes."

"Okay. You are right. I can walk."

"Okay, we will help you down onto the gurney."

The rescue people helped Kylie out the backdoor of the bus and she sat on the gurney. She was still shaking a little and felt nauseated.

"I think I need to lie down."

"Okay, here you go."

The blueshirts gently guided her down onto the gurney and they placed her legs on the stretcher. Kylie laid back and they put the mask back on her face again and took her vitals.

"Her blood pressure is pretty low," one said.

"Start an IV."

Kylie felt a prick on her arm and a cool trickle went up her arm. She closed her eyes, fighting back the urge to vomit but soon found she couldn't. She pulled the mask off, "I'm going to be sick."

Instantly there was a container under her chin and she promptly threw up vigorously into it several times. The last few she sobbed as the tears and snot mixed with the vomit.

"It's okay, let it go." the blueshirt said.

Kylie felt movement. They were on the way to the emergency room and hoped Peter or anyone else wasn't calling the police. She couldn't handle that scrutiny right now.

They took her to the hospital. By the time they arrived she was feeling much better and was sitting up sipping water against some pillows. The doctors check her over and came to the conclusion that the medication and the stress of her argument with her boyfriend triggered her to hyperventilate and she passed out. An anxiety attack the called it. She hadn't had one of those for a long time. They released her after a few hours and she took a cab home. She didn't mention the pepper spray or Peter specifically. She stuck with the argument story so she could keep flying under the radar. She felt foolish and weak.

Kylie stayed in for a couple weeks after that. Constantly looking ahead for any signs of Peter. After a while she determined he would keep clear of this area for a while. Kylie felt relieved as there were several nights when police sirens were in the street and she was sure they were coming to arrest her for assault. Eventually the feeling passed. He was going to hurt her, she did right.

Two

Her story was pretty grim. One of those typical moments when a trans woman is just an inch away from probable disaster. I wasn't quite sure what to think what could be worse. I saw the emotion on her face change as she told her story. I shook my head and thought how awful and settled in as this was going to be a long afternoon.

"That was pretty harsh. You are alright?"

"Yes, I am fine. Just something I used to do when I was younger, have anxiety attacks and pass out. That was before, before I started, started to transition. I was pretty messed up," She shook her head, "Too much information."

"No, it's okay. I understand."

You did that, right over there at that table?" I said.

"Yeah I did. Every time I come here I remember that."

"So what did you learn from that?"

Kylie, astonished, looked at me and

laughed.

"You do have some brass balls, you're too funny."

"I'm just trying to understand how this played out." I said playing naive.

"What did I learn? I learned don't say yes to weirdo stalkers in the bookstore, reading Feminist books," she said and then after a long pause, "I really learned to know more about the guy before disclosure. If I find out he is a hater, I finish the date and end it there."

"How do you find that out?"

"Telling them about the book I am reading with the transgender character in it," she said raising her eyebrows, pulling her e-reader out and waving at me. "You know, that and the little things I pay attention to, do you seem stable, kind, basically If I detect any asshole in you I cut it off."

I never really thought I was an asshole but does one ever really know that about themselves? I didn't want her to put me in that category and I felt I was already tipping the scales in that direction. I enjoyed being with her and didn't want whatever we had to end.

"You got me. My first reaction was bad but I'm not like your hater dude. I would maybe hate you later but it won't be because you have a penis. I will need to hear the other five."

I wasn't really sure if that was true or not but I did want to hear the rest of the stories. She was, after all, the most beautiful woman I had had the opportunity to get to know in a while. Not that I am desperate but I was longing for some companionship of late and since I met her, my life seemed a little brighter.

"Okay, number two," she said.

Dianne

The drink was poured with extra vodka, they all are at this nightclub. Ice to the top of an 18 ounce plastic glass then the liquor is poured in until the glass is three quarters full, the mixer tops the drink off. Gay folk take their drinking seriously and so does Dianne.

She wore a simple white loose tank top and baggy jeans, with boxer shorts sticking up in the back. No bra, her small breasts poked at the front of the shirt and the tank hung down in the arms enough most of breast was exposed from the side as she lifted her drink. Her short hair was cut close to her head and her arms showed a feminine musculature that was well defined and taught. She had a hard masculine edge to her though like the tough girl characters in zombie movies.

Kylie spotted Dianne from the other side of the bar near the windows. She was sitting with a friend from the gender group meeting.

In the recent weeks after her friend turned 21, they had been going out to the clubs together and dancing on weekends and were becoming a familiar fixture at 'that' side of the bar.

Dianne was watching the girl with the trans woman. She was beautiful, and was just the kind of girlie girl she was looking for. Kylie looked over at her. She stared her down and smiled as she sipped her drink through her straw.

Kylie was fortunate that she started transitioning late in her teens by the time she was 23 the hormones had transformed her into a young beautiful woman. Her body spared the ravages of testosterone, she was one of the 'passable' trans women in the gender group that met at the local LGBT community center. Though she was passable as female everywhere but the doctor's office, she did not feel ready for gender correction surgery. He own journey was continuing and she felt that she would do an injustice to herself by altering her sex organs at this stage in her life. She had desires. Desires for not only love and companionship but for sex and to discover where sex would lead her if given the opportunity.

Dianne was presenting an opportunity and Kylie was attracted to her. As she watched Dianne across the gulf of the bar she could also see that she was also interested. It was only a matter of time.

Dianne flagged down the bartender, she leaned up and said something close to his ear, then looked again at Kylie with a smile. He walked over and set a shot glasses upside down at their drinks.

"Hey girls, Dianne wants to buy you a cocktail," he said.

Dianne knew one of girls across the bar was trans but was not sure about the other prettier one. She did not care, as she felt an immediate attraction for her and was determined to find out one way or another, preferably by pulling her panties off in her bed later tonight. Dianne was on the prowl, it had been a while since her most recent relationship meltdown and was particularly horny tonight, even if the girl might have a dick. She wasn't one of those women who thought trans women were men 'pretending' to be women in some misogynistic plot to perpetuate a male dominated society. She saw them as other women.

Kylie looked over at her.

"Thanks. You should join us."

Dianne shouted across the bar, "What?!"

"I said thanks and come join us!" Kylie yelled back.

"I can't hear you! Come over here!" She actually could tell what she said but pointed at her ear anyway. She wanted to make her come to her.

Kylie could not understand anything over the loud music and the din of people talking. She just shrugged. Dianne waved her over.

"I'll be right back," she told her friend.

Her friend scowled a bit, "Sure leave me, see if I care," then laughed, "No go girl, she has been giving you the stink eye all night, and she is cute, like a skinny little dude."

Kylie walked around the bar through the crowd and stood next to Dianne. She stood half a head over her but she had on heels, still Dianne's presence was large despite her small frame. She looked up at Kylie.

"Hi, I'm Dianne, I got you and your friend the drinks."

"Yes, thanks much. I'm Kylie and she is Becky."

Kylie waved at Becky and she waved back and turned back to talk to some boys that were standing around her.

"You look hot in that dress." Dianne said abruptly.

"Ahhh, thanks and I like your look."

"Thanks, I've seen you here a few times before and wanted to get to know you. You seem like a fun person to get to know."

"Yeah, We caught eyes a few times. I've haven't seen you with anyone lately?"

"I broke up with my girlfriend. Sucks, but I am free now. What about you?"

"No one special. A few friends I hangout with but nothing serious."

"I got ya. Want to go dance? The floor is filling up. I think it is time to get sweaty."

"I'd love to, let me change my shoes real quick, I got some flats in my purse."

"Alright, cool, I'll be near that pillar over there." She pointed to the left of the dance floor.

"Okay, I'll be out there in a bit," Kylie said and left to change shoes.

Kylie was eager to party tonight, she hadn't cut loose for sometime. Mostly her and Becky would hang out at the bar drinking and would occasionally send some time on the dance floor but usually it was pretty subdued. The DJ was throwing down some pretty deep tracks and the beat was working her up some. Becky wasn't a big dancer and she always had to coax to spend anytime on the floor with her. Kylie had seen Dianne on several occasions dancing with her girlfriend. She obviously loved to dance and let her passions out on the dance floor. Kylie wanted to be on the receiving end of that passion for a change, to let herself go and forget about being trans, work and just disappear in the beat and the body of another.

Kylie dug her shoes out her purse Becky was tending and replaced her heels with the more marathon dance worthy ballet flats.

"Watch my purse okay, I am going dancing. If you have to check it at the coat check, for me okay?"

"Okay honey no problem, see you on the dance floor later, squeeze some ass for me too, okay?"

"Okay."

Kylie pecked her on the cheek and pranced off around the bar through the crowd. She had on a tight sheath dress that hugged her slim frame she didn't wear a bra and her breasts were nicely outlined in the dress. She had a tight thong on that kept her penis tucked up tight so it didn't show any bump on the front of the dress. Her golden brown hair was bundled up high with bangs and a few strands falling loosely to frame her face. She worked her way to the pillar in the dance floor and saw Dianne dancing solo to the thumping house music pouring from the speakers that lined the perimeter of the dance floor.

Kylie approached Dianne and she danced over to her and draped her arms over her shoulders and slowly gyrated her hips. They were now about the same height, Kylie put her hand on Dianne's hips and they began to match each other's movements.

They danced to the ebb and flow of the music mixed to perfection by the DJ, the rise ad fall of tension filled the space and the crowd began to build on the dance floor.

Kylie and Dianne at times danced in their own worlds to the trance inducing music filled with heavy beats that forced the body to move. As the tension built in the music the low end would drop out and a rise of white noise mixed with clacking electronic beats brought the girls together. Dianne wrapped her arms around Kylie as she arched her back and leaned backwards letting her arms drape to the floor, She was nearly looking backwards as Dianne kissed her under her chin and down her neck. Sparkling chills shot through Kylie as she let Dianne kiss her down further the open neckline of her dress, she slipped a shoulder off her dress and continued kissing her should and down the top of nearly exposed breast. Kylie rose up and met her mouth with hers and they engaged in a deep open mouth kiss as Dianne grabbed her ass with both hands and pulled her into her.

The music climaxed and the bass dropped, they broke and started dancing again. They wove into and around each other holding and releasing mixing kisses and sexual poses that foreshadowed what was to come in a few hours. Kylie knew she would go home with her tonight. So she needed to make sure Dianne knew who she was dealing with.

They came together kissing again on another transition in the beats. Kylie took Dianne's hand and pulled it down and up the hem of her short dress she placed her hand palm over her now straining penis trapped in the tight thong. As she could feel her hand discover that she had a penis, she looked into to her eyes. Dianne was just coolly looking back as she squeezed her then stroked the shaft that was tucked up under her. They kissed again and returned to dancing.

Dianne passed through the moment of disclosure without a blink. Kylie thought that she must have already read her and was undeterred. There are some women to define themselves as lesbian that treat trans woman as women. They look past genital based identity and see the person rather than the dick. This was true with Dianne, Kylie was not going to be the first t-girl she fucked and it wouldn't be her last.

Kylie was open to a fling or a one night stand it was just one of the ways to forming a long term relationship, probably not the best, but certainly it was better to be with someone than not. It had been a long time since Kylie was sexual with anyone. A long dry spell would be an accurate analogy in her case.

Kylie's last encounter was nearly a year ago an awkward drunken attempt with her now friend Becky. Before that not since college and the spree of anonymous Internet and sex club hookups prior to her fully assuming her female identity. Her past had some skeletons and they were all wearing strap-ons or lingerie.

"Do you want to come back to my place?" Dianne said in her ear.

They were taking a break back at the bar with Becky, both were wet with perspiration after nearly two hours of dancing. Becky was drunk and had latched onto a cute young man, so she was set for the night.

Kylie looked over at Becky and pointed at Dianne then herself and nodded.

Becky smiled, "Whore!" she yelled and laughed. "Go, I'm fine, I will be well taken care of tonight."

Kylie leaned over back to Dianne and kissed her.

"One more drink and then let's go." she said.

Dianne grinned as Kylie stood up and took

the glasses off the table. As she turned to walk by, Dianne was face level with her ass.

"Hold on!"

She reached up her dress and rubbed her naked butt cheeks, pulling her dress up, showing the table of people her ass with the thong.

"Look at that hot ass!" she said, and slapped one of the cheeks lightly.

Kylie laughed looking at the people all staring at her ass. She stuck it out and wiggled it back and forth dropping her slinky dress back down over her ass and continued to the bar.

"I am so tapping that tonight." Dianne boldly declared.

***

Noon seemed to come very early. Kylie woke laying in a large bed wrapped among a sheet and blanket. She looked over and saw a back with a large tattoo of a dragon running down the side with smaller birds and fish swirling around it. It was beautiful. She reached over and rubbed the cool brightly colored skin. The person stirred and rolled over, slowly opening her eyes. Dianne smiled, reached up and cupped Kylie's cheek with her hand. Kylie bent down and kissed her.

"I gotta go. I work at one."

"Okay," Dianne said and she fell back into her pillow and went back to sleep.

Kylie rose and found her few items of clothing spread around the room. Tossed them into a chair and went to the bathroom. She urinated naked standing at the toilet then washed her hands and face. She put her clothes back on watching Dianne. She was back asleep.

I guess I will let myself out. She thought.

She didn't get Dianne's number and she didn't ask her for one either. It seemed that it was one of those night that is best left to a pleasant one night stand. Two people simply wanting to share a night of intimacy with no expectations or disappointment. It was familiar territory for Kylie so she knew the routine. Leave, don't say goodbye and you will run into them again and maybe hookup another time, if you both are free; acquaintances with benefits.

She walked down the few flights of stairs

she couldn't find her flats so her heels clacked in the cavernous stairwell. She exited the building and was on the street. A few people were walking past they glanced briefly and went on. She walked to the corner to determine where she was as she pulled out her phone and brought up the map and located her position.

"Shit. I'm going to be late."

She walked quickly to the nearest bus stop and joined the few people waiting. She looked over and saw a girl about her age. Still in a nightclub dress, with evening makeup slightly decayed. She was carrying her heels and a small clutch, she had on a pair soft flats. She saw Kylie look at her. They both smiled and shrugged with unspoken knowledge that they both had great sex just a few hours before.

She trundled aboard the bus, took a seat and called her work.

"Hi, this is Kylie, I'm way across town, I'm gonna be an hour late."

Three

I have to admit I was a little aroused as she told her story. Certainly I was even more interested in her now and it's only been a few days.

"So you like girls too." I said.

"Yes I do. Is that a problem?" she said.

"Well not particularly, unless it means that you would rather be in a relationship with a woman instead of a man."

"You didn't ask that question. You asked me if I liked girls and I said yes. You didn't ask me if I wanted to be monogamous with a woman."

"Fair enough. Do you want to be monogamous with another woman, are you a lesbian?"

"I don't see it as an either or question so I can't answer. I would probably be monogamous with the person I'm in love with. If they want to have a third in bed once in a while I am not opposed to that either."

"So you are a swinger?"

"Oh for fuck sake, really?"

She looked at me like I was the dumbest thing on the planet.

"What? Isn't that what you call people that jump in naked piles with strangers and fuck each other?"

"I guess, but I am not a swinger. I don't go around jumping in naked piles and go hanging out with wrinkled old couples in seedy motels with a feather duster up my ass."

I laughed at the mental image of her on all fours.

"Okay, okay, lets just leave that alone, I concede that you are not a swinger."

"Lets just say my sexuality is open but I love who I love, male, female or other." She said.

"Others, like yourself?"

As soon as I said that I knew I pissed her off. She jumped on that immediately.

"I am a woman. Not an 'other'."

"I know I shouldn't of said that, sorry."

"Well you did and that is twice now you screwed up. Try three and see what happens."

She folded her hands and was quite upset. I did my best to smooth things over.

"Come on, I am trying to understand all this you know. I am not exactly up on my politically correct terminology to use when having coffee with a trann-transgender person."

She raised an eyebrow as I stumbled over 'transgender' almost saying 'tranny' instead, I smiled and she saw I was learning and shook her head slowly.

"So what about number three?" I asked.

She just sat there staring at me then sighed.

"Number three. This one is bad, for me anyway." she said.

"Are you sure to want to tell me? If you don't that is okay."

"No you got me started and you want to learn, this will show I can fall in love and I can be hurt."

Jack

The apartment was small, a combined kitchen, dining and bed room, with a bathroom and large dressing room with clothes rack behind French doors. A classic early twentieth century studio apartment. Kylie moved in two weeks before and had settled into the small space, adapting it as her living quarters and home office.

A small desk sat in one corner where a large flat panel monitor sat, her display for working, for Internet, watching movies and porn. She had a table, bought at a thrift store with two chairs. Not that she was expecting company anytime but *just in case* was a good scenario to adopt. Her bed was a folding foam pad big enough for one and a half people, when not being slept in it could fold into a low chair, that you slide out of if you sat in it.

A month or so had passed when finally she was greeted in the hallway by a neighbor. He was a nice looking guy, about six foot tall, he was always carrying his bicycle into his apartment. Kylie was just coming out of her apartment when he was trying to unlock the door while holding onto a bag of groceries, a backpack and his bike. She said hi as she passed and he was about to say something when the bike began to fall as he released it momentarily to adjust his grip on the backpack. Kylie caught the bike and prevented a major disaster of a dropped grocery bag with eggs and other breakable items.

"Whoa thanks. That would have been bad," he said.

"You're welcome, do need a hand?"

"Yeah could you? Take the wine from under my arm and the bag if you could."

Kylie took the bottle of wine and his back pack and wheeled the bike in through the door.

"Come on in, just set that stuff on the table."

Kylie stepped in only as far as she dared and set the items on the table. He quickly leaned his bike against the wall and placed the groceries on the table as well.

"You must be the new person in 312. I saw you move in the other day. I'm Jack, Jack Carter."

"Hi, Kylie Hasting."

He held out his hand and Kylie shook it.

"Nice to meet you. Thanks much for the help. You're a life saver. I almost dropped the groceries and that would have been a mess and would meant no breakfast for a week for me, nearly broke again."

"I know how that is."

"For sure, I guess it is why we live where we do."

Kylie didn't lead on that she was actually pretty comfortable with money from her job and chose this place because she just likes living small.

"Well I gotta go catch a bus downtown, I have a meeting at 3:30."

"Hey I do too, I can ride with. I have to go to the DMV, I hate going there. Sucks up the whole day."

"Well okay, I'll see you down there," she said.

"Yeah I'll be right down I just gotta throw a clean shirt. If you wait just a minute I'll walk down with you."

He ducked into his dressing room and before Kylie could say anything he emerged wearing a fresh blue tee shirt and a wide grin.

"See, no problem. Lets go."

Kylie led him out the door, she paused as he locked up, twisting the key in three locks. She waited for him because it seemed rude to do otherwise and she was happy to be around someone again. She hadn't really talked to anyone outside of work and the night club in weeks.

They walked together the two blocks to the bus stop. The streets were busy on Friday's with people leaving work early for the weekend and people stocking up for the weekend. As they walked he chattered away to her, telling her when and who moved in if they were nice or mean. He even went on about the laundry machine sin the basement and told her which ones to avoid. At one point she found herself laughing at his amusing stories of everyday life in the apartment building.

He was nice looking, firmly built and was

polite. A good combination for a prospective boyfriend she thought. Plus having him down the hall in the apartment could be a good thing if they hit it off but it could be nightmarish if they don't. Kylie thought it best to start out as friends, after all, he was as straight as an arrow so it seemed. So she would have to tell him about her pretty quick if it looked like there was any romance going forward.

For right now, Kylie was happy to spend a bus ride with her new building friend. She laughed at his jokes and he listened to her stories. She was so at ease with him it was almost alarming. At one point as he was showing her something funny on his phone she held on to his arm and leaned against him. Her breasts pushing against his shoulder. He felt them on him and he looked over at her and smiled.

His stop was approaching and he looked a little sad that they would part. He quickly recovered and said, "Hey you want to meet later? I know this cool little pub we could have a few beers and maybe shoot pool or something."

"I thought you were broke?" she said.

"I am but not for cocktails. I have a budget I stick to and I haven't used much of my party budget this week. So it's cool."

"A party budget. So now you are an organized guy?"

"Priorities my dear, gotta keep things prioritized."

"Well that sounds good, I am headed further downtown to the Simmons Tower, I have a meeting at work and should be done by four so."

"That would work just hop the bus back and meet me at the DMV. I'll probably still be in line, its just up ahead at the next stop. Here shoot me a text real quick."

He gave her his number and she sent him a text as he was leaving the bus. He waved as the bus continued on. She held her hand up and smiled as he disappeared from view.

Her meeting was long and it was almost five before she could break away and text him. He replied he was still five people from the window and not to worry.

She exited the building and boarded a bus that had just pulled up heading in the direction she needed to go. It was a short trip in the heavy traffic the bus was crowded with tired sweaty people. Many silent and looking exhausted from long work week. Others appeared ready to party early on the Friday. They pulled up to the government center and she exited with a dozen or so others. She followed the signs and was about to enter, when Jack came out the doors. He grinned a wide beaming smile when he saw her, his face showing without a doubt he was happy to see her. She laughed a little at his reaction. It was so odd, having someone so excited to see you, almost like a puppy.

"Awesome! You made it. How was your meeting?"

"Oh god it was dull, they piled more work for me, I'll be busy most of the next week and through the following to meet the deadline. But they will pay me a shitload and I'll have some downtime for a week or so, it all balances out."

"That's cool. Come on, the pub is just a block or so away."

They cut through the government center courtyard to the opposite side of the block, then crossed the street. She saw the pub, The

Iron Monger an English style pub that wasn't a dive but wasn't a chain. They walked in, it was busy for Friday happy hour, and the bar was full but some tables were still available outside..

"Let's sit out front." he suggested.

The picked a high table near the building and sat on the stools. A server showed up immediately and presented them with the beer list and cocktail menu. They quickly picked pints of the local brew.

"This place is busy," Kylie said.

"Yeah it always is around this time but the happy hour people leave in droves in an hour and then the Friday night crowd starts to filter in. We'll be able to shoot some pool after our beer."

No sooner had he said 'beer' and the server was back with two English pints of the golden beer. They both sipped at the same time watching each other.

"Oh that's tasty," she said.

"How cool, a girl that likes beer. What are you from Wisconsin or something?"

Kylie laughed loudly. "What just because I

like beer?"

"Well yeah, most of the time if a girl drinks anything other than light beer, she is probably from Wisconsin, at least that was how it was in school anyway."

"Well if you must know. Yes I am from Wisconsin."

"HAH! I knew it! I thought I recognized a little of that 'you betcha' accent."

"Yes I grew up in Black River Falls and went to school in Madison. Go Badgers!" She said and pulled another drink from her pint.

"Oh uhoh, well you know we can't watch football together."

"No don't say it," she said.

"I am afraid so, I'm a Buckeye."

"Well I can see this is going to be a battle. Buckeyes vs. Badgers for the Big Ten post graduation, pool title, oh buy the way, I grew up with a pool table in my basement."

"Oh you are so on," he said.

Jack was so filled with energy several groups of guys came in and they all stopped to talk with him. He had endless fun explaining how he met his new neighbor and that she was a Badger many would groan and curse in a mock rival way. Mostly he lavished attention on her introducing her to his friends. They were all your typical young single guys and were more than eager to make her acquaintance.

"Hey grab a table and lets play some partners." He told the most familiar group of old college friends of his.

"We'll have to hold off on our world championship and we'll take those guys on."

"Sounds like fun."

Kylie watched him closely, he was showing the longer they were together, the more he was attracted to her. She needed to play this carefully else she could get in real trouble. This was going to be a difficult relationship. She could see that his buddies were pretty much good old boys not the redneck kind but the 'bro' kind, they were cute and friendly but they were also dripping with testosterone and as it appeared, straight.

Kylie's gaydar pretty much shutdown the minute they walked into the pub. She didn't, hear any disparaging talk about gay folk and looking around the pub there was quite a mix of people present. So she went with a positive assumption that the bar did not tolerate any haters or bigots. But these were straight guys and Jack was as all American as a guy could be. He would no doubt, expect his girlfriend to not have a penis.

They finished a few drinks and played a few games of pool with Jack's bar buddies. Kylie noticed they seemed to appreciate her bending over the pool table or looking down her shirt as she stretched to take a shot. Jack sat on a stool and smiled at her as she nearly ran the table. After it was clean she was not to be beaten Jack's friends wandered off to play darts and watch a sporting event coming on one of the dozens of televisions.

"Well should we take off?" Jack asked.

Kylie just finishing the last of her drink looked at the empty bottom of the glass and said, "Yeah, work tomorrow and if I have another I'll probably end up drinking the rest of the night. So yes, lets take the bus back to the apartment."

Jack led the way out of the now crowded pub. The emerged out on the street. Jack politely guiding her with his hand on the small of her back as she exited first.

"Lets walk a few blocks the catch a bus. I always like walking downtown. Its fun to watch people."

"Sure," Kylie said as she took his arm.

She liked Jack, he was cute, funny and polite.

They walked slowly along the street to a causal observer they appeared to be a couple, based on the ease in how they interacted. Kylie watched Jack as he was pointing out some of the historical buildings and talked about the downtown had changed.

"This whole area was really seedy," he said. "When I was a kid we would come down here on our bikes and ride past the hookers and trannies that were hanging around the gay bars that were on this block. There are still some bars but the rest was cleaned up."

"Trannies?" Kylie asked.

"Yeah you know, transsexuals? I guess I should use the proper term. Gotta be PC you know, don't want to offend anyone," he said as he made 'air quotes' with his fingers.

"So what do you think of all that?" Kylie

asked.

"What, downtown changing?"

"No, *transsexuals* and gay folk." Kylie said.

"Oh well, I guess people do what they do. Doesn't really matter to me, two of the dudes we played pool with are gay if that is any example."

Kylie cocked her head, "I didn't get that at all from those guys, but now that you mention it they did seem friendly to each other. What about you? You ever—you know—with guys?"

Jack laughed. "Me? Maybe, kid stuff, but If I was totally attracted to guys I wouldn't be here with you, but sadly, I am not trendy, just an everyday boring dude that mostly likes girls.

"That is pretty bold. I mean do you always tell girls you date you have been with guys before?"

"Whoa, I didn't say I had been with guys."

"Well you implied it, so have you?"

"Yes a couple times."

"So have you ever told anyone?"

"No not really but I guess I would with someone who I really cared for. No secrets you know. I just haven't met anyone like that, until now."

Kylie paused her questioning and thought about what he said.

"You think I am special enough to entrust that information with?"

"I didn't plan to tell you but somehow here we are talking about it. So that must be something, don't you think?" He said.

Kylie smiled partially and nodded. She decided she would take a chance and tell him now.

They walked quietly along the old facades of brick and stone buildings that ringed the modern city center. Kylie paused at some shop windows and was commenting on some antiques in a window when she asked him.

"What if you met a girl and found out she was considered male at birth?"

"Odd question. What do you mean considered?"

"I mean they gave the child a M on the birth certificate but later that was exactly accurate. You know trans people."

"That's cool, I guess. How would I know?"

"Let me rephrase, what if you met a girl and she told you she was trans?"

Jack stopped and looked at her.

She reached out and took his hand, "Come on keep walking," she said as she pulled along.

Jack began to look closely at Kylie. His brow was furrowed and his eyes were scanning her face, hair. He lifted her hand to his and compared his with hers.

Kylie smiled back and shrugged her shoulders raising, her eyebrows.

"You—," he stopped.

Kylie nodded as he fell behind still holding her hand. She stopped and was looking back, holding hands. He looked at her and then their hands and back to her face, slowly a smile broke and he took the two steps forward.

"I guess if I was attracted to her and we got a long I would say anything. It doesn't change who she is right now, does it?"

Kylie took his other hand and she faced him. "No it doesn't change who she is right now."

They continued down the street. Kylie reached up and put her arm across his back to his far shoulder and tipped her head against him, touching his shoulder for a moment.

***

Kylie felt loose. Loose, not like falling apart but more like a comfortable pair of yoga pants. She felt there was some purpose and reason for her to press through her day beyond survival. She had someone in her life now. Another living breathing person that is right here in real life. One she can touch and talk to without the use of a computer or phone. Jack was a 'real life' person and was her person.

They reached the river and turned up the river walk and decended some stairs to the railing, they stood watching the river traffic as it glided by. Up the walk there were several cafes and pubs bustling with customers. She felt a hand on her shoulder and she turned and met his eyes. His hand moved to her cheek and he leaned in tilting his heard sightly and kissed her lips with a short light kiss. Kylie felt a rush of warmth cascade down her body and she responded to his kiss with another.

A slow, reluctant kiss at first but it ended with a flush of warmth and excitement for each and turned into a long embrace.

Jack laughed a little after the kiss.

"Wow, that was totally not what I expected."

"How do you mean?"

"Well, It was different. I was expecting something sorta more, you know."

"Guy like?"

"Well yeah I guess, but I didn't want to go there."

"I understand."

Jack took her hand, "I didn't really know what to expect I guess and when I felt your lips and my hand on your waist. Whatever I was thinking about you and what I expected simply disappeared. I didn't care."

"I think I know. I felt something a little like that too. Maybe it is still there."

Kylie took his other hand and stood in front of him. He put his hands on her hips and leaned in a kissed her again sliding his hand up her back. They kissed a several long precious seconds.

"Dinner tomorrow?"

"Love to. Walk me to my bus stop?"

"Sure." Jack laughed knowing the were riding to the same building on the same bus. But It was fun to play along.

They turned and walked the half a block to the bus stand. Kylie leaned against the glass loosely hanging onto Jack's hand.

They didn't talk much as they waited the few moments for the bus.

The bus pulled up and the doors opened. Jack and Kylie flashed their bus passes to the driver and walked to the back and sat in a seat. The people and the glass store fronts started to blur as the roar of the bush increased to near jet levels.

"You know living in the same building could be a problem."

"Or convenient." Kylie said with a smile.

"That is the problem I am talking about. You see I love to cook so I just would not want you slaving in the kitchen over me every day."

"Do you do laundry too?"

"As a matter of fact I do. My mother taught me. Been washing my own clothes since I was ten."

"Well that's good. You know how to read tags then?"

"Yes I have mastered those cryptic tiny symbols. You know the slash through the dryer and iron. I got those."

"Good. Just in case some of my lingerie ends up in your bedroom you will know what to do with it."

"Absolutely. If it comes to that I know how to wash teddies, bustiers and those really skimpy panties, read the tag how tough could it be? But hay, I draw the line though at the toilet seat. It goes back up in my bathroom."

"You shouldn't have to worry about that."

"Now that sounds exciting. But now, lets not get ahead of ourselves."

"Oh, no absolutely, go slow approach, I

totally agree." Kylie said with a genuine shock.

"We have to at least wait," Jack paused and whispered close to her ear then pecked her cheek, "wait until we get off this bus."

Kylie grinned and for the first time in a long time felt that rush of excitement of what lies next. They rode for a while in silence and the bus pulled close to the original stop that they walked to from their apartment building. They stood and Kylie pulled the stop requested line.

"So you sure, this is what you want to do?" She said.

"Yes," Jack said and bent down and kissed her as she looked up at him, "How about you come knock on my door at 10:30 tonight. I'll have a late night snack and a nice bottle of wine. We can sit and watch a scary movie."

"I'd like that."

"Wear something comfy. I wear drawstring pants and a tee most of the time I am home."

"Okay. Should I bring toothbrush?"

"If you don't I have a new one in my medicine cabinet."

"Is this a sleepover?"

"I hope so." Jack said.

Four

She finished her story and looked a little sad. She had been stirring her now cold coffee with a spoon and uncermoniously dropped it on the table then sighed.

"That was a sweet story. No unhappy tragedy there," I said.

"We ended up together, for six months. Then he got laid off, he found a new job pretty quick but he had to leave the city. I don't blame him, it was a good opportunity and we —well we were just not ready for one another I guess."

"He liked you though?"

"I want to think so but, I think I knew he liked the idea of being with a trans woman. He certainly enjoyed the sex—I did too for that matter. But I don't think he was in it for the long run."

"So he wasn't going to take you home to meet mom then?"

"Yeah no, probably not."

She seemed defeated and I felt maybe it

was time for a change of venue.

"What do you say we take a walk. There is a park a few blocks ahead, overlooking the river, nice place to sit."

"That sounds nice. I could use some fresh air. This trip down memory lane you have me on is not exactly happy fun time, but it's important."

"I understand. I'll go pay the bill. I need to use the restroom too."

"I'll be here."

I walked over to the counter and found the server, paid the bill and made a quick rest stop. As I came back out she was looking out the window. Her hair was shining in the sun and her face was silhouetted in the window. I saw how beautiful she was again. I held up my phone and took a picture of her then walked over to her.

"We're all set, ready?"

"Let's go," she said.

We exited the coffee shop the sun was tipping beyond it's midday zenith, the air was warm, it was a good day to have a beautiful girl by my side. I reached down and took her hand in mine. She looked up, her eyes, a little wet blinked and she gave me a half smile.

I held up my phone and showed her the photo.

"You don't mind do you? I just thought that made a nice photo."

"No that's okay. It's a good picture. Send it to me later," she said.

"Sure."

We walked quietly for a minute or so. I could see that she was lost in some thought.

"It must be hard being like you, always wrestling with your past and your future," I said.

She turned and looked at me. The sun cast shadows of her hair that framed her face and she smiled.

"That is observant of you."

"I can see that in you now. I thought it was just you being mysterious and aloof but I see now there is much more depth beyond first impression."

"I fascinate you then?"

"I would be lying if I said you didn't, you do, but in a way that makes me want to know everything about you."

"Really?"

I nodded my head and we continued walk to the entrance of the park that was in the distance yet.

"So who is next on your list?"

"Melissa."

"A girl?"

"Yes, a trans woman like me."

"Is this story good or bad?"

"Well lets just say they are all good, I learn something new about myself with each one."

"Okay then, fire away."

Melissa

Kylie clicked on the button to open the video display of Melissuck4U. Her profile picture was pretty striking and she was broadcasting. After a few seconds the screen came to life and Melissuck4U was sitting at the camera wearing a tank top. She looked bored.

Among the random strangers that were asking her to show various parts of her anatomy Kylie typed 'Hello' in the chat window. The girl in the video window raised her eyebrow and looked to the side. She moved her mouse and some clicking could be heard. The glow of the screen flashed a few times on her face and a wry smile appeared on her face.

A chat window popped up on Kylie's desktop.

'Hey girl. Like your pics. What's up?'

Kylie typed a reply.

'Nothing just surfing, saw your profile and thought I would say hi.'

'Kewl, I am bored. Nothing but dickheads in here today.'

'That is usually the case.'

'I see we are from the same place. You go to club Visage? I think I've seen you there before with a queer chick, you were dancing super hot with her.'

'Yeah I go there, and that was probably me,' Kylie typed.

'I'm Melissa.'

'Kylie.'

'So if I see you there this weekend wanna have a drink with me?'

'Sure sounds fun. I usually sit on the back side of the bar by the windows.'

'Oh right, the trans spot. I see you like girls like us.'

'I am one of the girls like us.' Kylie said.

Melissa blinked a couple of times and her eyes darted to another part of her screen. She clicked a few times and the light in her face flickered.

'wtf'

'wtf what?' Kylie typed.

'I thought you were cis. Girl you look good.'

'Oh thanks, is that a problem?'

'No fuck no, girl I play the field, can catch or receive.'

'I know I've seen a few of your shows here.'

'Did you tip?'

'lol, no.'

'cheap bitch. Lol'

'ikr, I'll buy some shots then.'

Kylie laughed to herself.

'gotta go, I gotta live one. Back to work. Hey, I'll be at the club Thursday for the shows. Come down and we can hang out.' Melissa typed.

'sounds good, see you there.'

Kylie saw Melissa's video screen go dark as she disconnected for a private session with a paying customer. Lots of girls supplement their income with private video shows over the Internet. Kylie keeps that in her back pocket just in case her employment situation changes. It was a little smarmy but it was

100% safer than the alternative.

Kyle felt a little guilty, she had sort of half stalked Melissa after she recognized her at the club one night. She had watched a few of her free shows on the web and after a little research discovered she lived in town. Seeing her recently was an added plus. Kylie was very attracted to her and after her last relationship ended with a whimper she had been craving some sexual company. She wasn't usually attracted to sex working trans girls but Melissa being local she thought It would be fun to hang out with her.

She knew that girls like her come with a lot of baggage. She lately recognized that this was simply unfair and the only reason she didn't make more friends in the trans community was from her own self loathing that she still had issues in overcoming. She had to let that go.

Once she acknowledged her own shortcomings and with a few encounters of her own. She was able to let herself be okay with who she was she then able to start letting herself accept others. She knew she was far from perfect. With a few years of transition and lots of hours of therapy she was finally comfortable being queer, with being the 'T' in the LGBT.

For a long time she felt she was above all that. She was at times in her life disgusted and angry but once she realized those attitudes came from her inability to accept who she was, she was able to heal. She was no longer ashamed of herself, or her desires. She accepted the community that accepted her long ago. At times she has moments of guilt that bear down her at unexpected times. It was a heavy burden to carry all those years and one that is not easily set aside. Though the occurrences are growing less frequent. She still finds herself unable to rise to the day and spends the day in bed, despondent and weepy for her past.

She became friends with an older trans woman, Emma, though a service organization her therapist suggested. Emma was the first trans women that she got to know and once she was able to see past the person's outer appearance and her own binary gender conditioning, she saw a beautiful, kind and compassionate person. That person helped her to see her faults clearly and how her irrational self hatred was effecting her life and those around her. Kylie assisted Emma on a few projects and they struck up a friendship that provided Kylie her first female friend role model. She would host picnics at her house and she recruited Kylie's help with her garden, a common love they shared. Their friendship was unfortunately brief.

One night after returning from preparing dinner at the LGBT youth shelter she broke down as she rode in bus. She had received a call from the therapist. She said that Emma had passed away yesterday. She died of a stroke in her backyard while gardening. She was 68 years old.

It was that moment that Kylie's life began to change and the person who she was had begun to tear away the layers of resistance she had constructed over the years.

As she stumbled into her apartment, Kylie slumped against the door and wept. The mixture of healing and the influence of massive doses of estrogen were changing her dramatically. Her friend was gone and she felt the pain of that loss with striking clarity.

Emma taught her to go beyond yourself and to reach out others and let yourself go. She recalled what Emma always said to her, "If you don't let go the past, you will never be able to hold onto anything in the future."

Emma taught her to let go as she did a number of other young trans women.

Because of the experiences with her therapist and letting herself become friends with others, Kylie broke the cycle of self destruction and was able to open herself to new experiences and risk. Risks not only of rejection but of acceptance and love.

Because of Emma, Kylie was able to meet people and see them not someone to fear for what might happen, but as someone to embrace for what may happen. Love and kindness can only be grasped when you let go of yourself and trust in others. That was a difficult lesson for Kylie to learn. So she was taking another chance by meeting Melissa at the club tomorrow night.

***

Kylie was stirring her drink and looking at her phone when she looked up and spotted Melissa standing across the corner of the bar.

"Haaaaay girl," she said and laughed.

Melissa slid around the corner of the bar and hugged Kylie lightly and they kissed each other's cheeks.

"Hi! You look terrific, that dress is so cute."

She raised her eyebrows and smiled, blushing a little.

"Thanks. God I so need a drink."

She sat in a bar stool next to Kylie and ordered a vodka and soda in a 'big girl glass'. She watched the bartender make her drink and then told Kylie, "I almost wasn't going to come out."

"Really, why?"

"Oh god, well lets just say things are complicated right now and I wasn't sure what you or I wanted."

"Sort of jumping ahead are you? I was thinking of maybe some drinks and some dancing would be fun," Kylie said.

"Oh I know, that is what I came to realize too. I'm actually nervous as hell. I'm sorry."

"It's okay, I know how that is."

"I know right, nobody said this shit gets any easier. I mean I am such a pussy. I can be totally naked shoving stuff up my ass for strangers yet, meeting someone I'm attracted to in real life for drinks is making me freak out."

"Well if it makes you feel better, I've seen you naked and I'm still here."

Melissa stared at her for a moment then laughed. "Oh fuck it, lets get some shots. Cherry bomb?"

Kylie nodded, "You are a pussy. How about Jager bombs."

The bartender brought her drink over and Kylie ordered a couple shots for them.

Kylie wondered what would happen tonight, based on past nights at the club, if that was any guide, they would be together at least for tonight.

I need some human contact, she thought.

The bartender brought the shots and the girls knocked them back with little effort.

Kylie watched Melissa. She moved with grace the belied her birth gender, her makeup was a little on the heavy side but well executed and was well suited to the club atmosphere, as was her cocktail dress.

"So do you have a day job?" Kylie asked. Just as she said it she regretted it. It was one of those subjects that more often than not goes badly.

"No I got fired after I came out trans. I worked as a desktop support rep for an old school manufacturing company in town."

"Oh, shit I'm sorry. We can drop that if it bothers you."

"No it's okay. I haven't had the chance to tell anyone really."

"Did they fire you because you were trans?"

Yeah I think so, they wouldn't say that but I had great reviews and a promotion recently. Not a few weeks after I talked to my boss and HR about being trans they found that my job performance was lacking and let me go. It was bullshit and I called them on it."

"What did they do?"

"Had security escort me out to my car. They wouldn't even let me get my stuff. They said If I came on the property they would call the sheriff and have me arrested for trespassing. They said they would bring my personal items to my house but I have yet to see that."

"Fuck that totally sucks."

"I know right they still have my travel mug. Fuck them. I have some resumes out and have a had a few bites, so I should be back at the day gig soon enough. Assholes, they really fucked me over and I really liked that mug. What about you?"

"Risk Analyst, I work remote from home mostly I do go in for meetings. They seem to be cool but they are a huge corp and so they are pretty inclusive."

"That's cool."

"I can check my job board and see if we have any positions, shoot me your resume if you want."

"Awesome, thanks."

Kylie, lost in thought at Melissa's work struggles compared them to her own. She had come out with little fanfare at her last job. At the same time she had been planning on freelancing and had already lined up a consulting firm to work with. Kylie benefited from having coding and business analyst skills that were in demand and she was able to line up work on her terms fairly easily as a result.

She watched Melissa scanning the crowd and sipping her drink. She saw that stress of job loss on her face and felt a pang of sadness for her and decided to change the subject and focus on having a good time.

"Work sucks lets forget it and party. Want to shoot some pool?"

"I am all for that. Pool lets. I love to bend over a stick." Melissa said.

"Hah. That's what she said."

"I know, right?"

They refreshed their drinks and walked to the back of the second level of the club where the pool tables and lounging bar were. It was around 10:30 so the night was just getting started. The girls settled into a few games of eight ball and soon attracted a couple of straight looking guys who put quarters up on the table.

"Looks like we can play teams." Melissa said.

"Indeed." Kylie smiled.

Melissa instantly started flirting with the guys. They at first were a little standoffish but soon Melissa had them laughing. One guy was holding on to the other's belt loop so Kylie assumed they were together. Kylie finished and broke her own rack. One of the boys took Melissa's pool cue and lined up a shot. He glanced over at Kylie, smiled and took a shot. He missed.

"You girls partying tonight?"

"Oh most likely. It's early yet."

"Yeah, Danny, my boyfriend and I, its our first time here. He just turned 21."

"Oh cool. So is it all that you expected."

He looked over at Melissa and then her and smiled. "It is."

"Cool it there young man." Kylie smiled and watched Melissa line up her shot. She stuck out her ass as she bent over and spread her thighs. Her dress rode up her thighs and that afforded the two young men a full view of her ass and panties, which made more than clear that she had a penis well tucked under her cocktail dress.

Kylie watched as the boys grinned and one hit the other on the shoulder. Melissa just turned and grinned then shot. She made the next four shots.

The girls beat the boys 2 out of 3 on the rubber match. That cost them a round of shots and the tab for post clubbing breakfast. Melissa and Kylie had found some party buddies. The four hung out drinking and taking shots around the back bar. There was a lot of laughter and partying stories. The boys shared how they met and commended the girls on being 'super hot messes'. After they had an ample buzz on and the dance floor was getting active they moved the party to the floor. The four spent the remainder of the night dancing with each other and around in the crowd on the floor.

Kylie and Melissa danced together most of the night. Taking breaks for cocktails and to use the bathroom.

Melissa had just finished touching up her mascara. She looked in the mirror twisting her head both ways and said, "So I think you should come over tonight. We seem to be needing each other right now. God knows I sure want to see you naked."

Kylie smiled and reached over and put her hand on her ass. "I am all for that."

Melissa leaned in and her lips parted just a small amount as she moved slowly forward to meet Kylie's lips. The kiss was brief and sweet. Melissa pulled back and smiled a little blushing.

"Ohmigod you are blushing. That is so cute," Kylie said.

Melissa just rolled her eyes and returned to her makeup. Stopping to watch Kylie watching her. Her hand was still on her ass. She finished her makeup, turned and took her hand.

"Come on lets go dance."

The girls walked out of the bathroom and Kylie took Melissa's arm and they cat-walked down the long hallway leading to the edge of the main floor ringed with booths and sofa pits.

They entered the floor and were enveloped in the warm cones of light sweeping the floor mixed with sparkles, multi-colored dots and lasers executing careful patterns creating flowers and other shapes. The music settled into a beat that allowed them to dance against each other and those around them.

Arms above their heads they twirled into the mist letting all the anxiety of the past and future slide away. They fell into a cascading filter sweep that ushered in the pounding kick drum and a new cycle of musical tension and release.

Melissa was dancing with her eyes closed just absorbing herself into the beat. She would open her eyes ever few seconds and reach out and touch Kylie, who would turn and press her body against hers. The liquor mixed with the beat and vibe of the mostly gay crowd swept them away for another hour.

After one particularly emotional build and release Kylie grabbed up Melissa and they draped themselves on each other and traded kisses as the music swirled into a new beat and tempo.

"I'm hungry. Lets beat the crowd and go get something to eat. The Basement Diner is open. They serve food until 3."

"Lets I'm starved."

It wasn't hard for Kylie to feel at ease with Melissa. She was like herself in so many ways. Yet was also different in others. They were walking towards the front door when they spotted the boys from earlier making out against the wall in alcove near the coat room. Melissa looked at them and smiled then held out her hand brushed it across their cheeks as they walked by. The boys broke their kiss and saw the girls and waved.

"We are going to the Basement, you want us to save you a seat?" Melissa said.

One of the boys looked over at the other and she saw a little head shake. Then the other grin.

"I think we are heading to my place. But thanks, next time."

His eyebrows raised and he refocused his attention on his lover.

"I think they would rather fuck." Melissa said to Kylie.

"Ya think? So would I."

"Bitch you ain't getting any of this until I get some food," Kylie said in an exaggerated manner.

"There ain't no tits on me. Oh, wait. Yes there is."

Melissa said as she rubbed her hands down her sides like a 50's starlet.

Kylie reached over and squeezed them.

"Hay! OW!"

The girls laughed and exited out the front door and crossed the street to the diner. There was already a line extending out the door. As they approached someone said, "45 minutes."

Melissa and Kylie's face drooped.

"Oh fuck this place. I have some left over roast chicken I was gonna make quesadillas with. Come over and we can snug at my place eat a 'dilla and I'll let you play with my dilla's." Melissa said.

Kylie smiled, "I can dig that. You drive?"

Melissa nodded, they locked arms and marched off to Melissa's car arm in arm.

***

The apartment was sparse, just a table with a couple of folding camp chairs, a ratty looking futon and coffee table. In the corner was a desk with three computers, a laptop and three monitors. Across from the desk in the opposite corner was a low bed with colorful pillows and spread with sheer drapes lining the perimeter. A bank of lights was set up and were obviously used to illuminate the scene. There was a small shelf next to the bed that had various pairs of high heel shoes, and sex toys neatly arranged in the shelves. Hanging on the wall above were various leather straps, whips, chrome chains and several hangers with a variety of lingerie neatly ordered on hangers. Kylie was staring at the scene.

"This is where the magic happens. I am sure you recognize some of my buddies."

"I do. Looks as sexy in real life as it does on the web."

"Wanna be a star?" Melissa said smiling.

"No. But thanks for asking. I'll keep my junk off the web for now."

"It's fun."

"Well yeah I am sure it is but the idea of the clips spreading around to all the tube sites sorta creeps me out."

"I think of that as free advertising. When you do it for money getting your clip on one of those sites is just like getting a review on a book site or music site. I got uploaded by this dude and I went ahead and gave the okay and filled in my contact stuff. I've been rocking with more business I can pick and choose when I work and what I do. The web has taken the danger out of a sex work. Sort of."

"I suppose. Still, I'm an old fashioned girl still."

Melissa brought a couple of cocktails over, handed one to Kylie and looped her arm around her back.

"Cheers."

They touched glasses and sipped, Kyle said, "I am glad you asked me out. It was sorta odd cause I know you have seen my free shows, but it is nice to know someone locally."

Kylie blushed a little. They were staring at each other, then cracked up laughing.

"Look at us laughing like a couple high schoolers. Come on lets loaf. I'll put some music on or something. Maybe later you and I can surf the web chats and tease the guys. Watch some cocks." Melissa said.

"Kylie thought about that as she sipped the drink. "Okay but I'm not taking anything off."

"No, no you don't have to we'll just chat, it will drum me up some more clients."

"Okay", Kylie said skeptically.

"Girl no worries. I won't make you do anything you don't want to do, promise."

"Well you couldn't anyway."

Melissa slid over to her and pulled Kylie against her, stared into her eyes and gently brushed her hair back. Then ran her finger across her lips then gently kissed them.

"Sure about that?" she said.

Kylie just grinned and kicked off her shoes and flopped on the brightly colored bed in her the video studio. Melissa put some music on one of the computers and then with another brought up several windows from different websites. In a few minutes they were broadcasting on five different websites and had over three thousand people watching them drink cocktails and listen to music.

Melissa leaned over and whispered in her ear, "Just having you here I will make five or six hundred dollars."

"People are paying to watch us drink?"

"Yup. See that window in the corner. That's my paypal account. I have it linked to the various sites and as people pay to see my cams a portion of the transactions goes into my paypal as pending. Non paypal accounts take more time and come monthly from the sites themselves."

"Jesus Melissa that is shit load of money for like nothing."

"I know right. Now if we had sex, multiply that by 5 or 6."

"Wow. That is crazy. People are so fucking horny."

"People are so fucking lonely. Here is one of my regulars. I'll bring him up." Melissa said.

She clicked on one of the names and in a minute a video window popped up. A private pay Skype call. They man was probably in his late fifties. He was very slim and sitting at his computer in a white oxford shirt.

"Morning love. You are looking lovely today and who is your adorable friend."

"Stan this is Kissy. She is one of my trans girl friends."

"Kissy it is ever so nice to meet you. Kissy that is a delightful name."

Kylie blushed and forced back yelling at

Melissa but instead she just smiled.

"Thank you, it is nice to meet you Stan."

"Well Melissa you caught me just as I was about pop, off to work. I have a bit of a drive this morning."

"You can't stay and watch me and Kissy?"

"No I'm sorry to disappoint but I have a schedule you know. But I still wouldn't mind a taste of what I was missing."

"Okay, Well here is a little bit you will like."

Melissa turned over to Kylie and took a drink of her drink then slowly moved to kiss her. Kylie met her lips and felt Melissa's tongue separate her teethe and she transferred the liquor from her mouth to Kylie's. Kylie choked a little then swallowed. She was thrilled knowing Stan was watching a kiss. She looked over at the camera then returned and kissed Melissa tenderly.

"Oh bravo, girls that is delightful. I am sorry I must run but I have to get up to make the train. Here is something for you dear. Bye now!"

"Bye Stan see you Friday?" Melissa said.

"With bells on and other things my love."

His screen went dark and a few seconds later her paypal account showed an incoming transaction of $133 dollars.

"See what I mean. Stan is super nice and he lives all alone and works like a dog all the time. He is horribly closeted and kinky. Only gets it up when he is being a total sub. He is one of my regulars. I think he is in some powerful position or something. He only shares his video with me. I guess he trusts me. I could record him and black mail but that is just immoral. I'm not like that."

Kylie finished off her drink, took Melissa's glass and got up.

"Another drink? I'll make them. I gotta pee too."

"No pee in mine please." Melissa said without emotion as she went back to checking her accounts on the web.

"Girl ewwww! I'm wasn't going to pee in them."

"Oh ok."

Kylie laughed her way to the small kitchen and set the glasses down and went to the small bathroom in the corner. She scanned around the tiny room to make sure there wasn't any cameras. There wasn't. She lifted the hem of her short dress up and pulled her penis out the side of her thong and let go a long relaxed piss.

She washed up and checked her make up and hair. It was a little frazzled but was still pretty hot. She went back out and made fresh drinks and turned back out into the small studio main room. Melissa had changed and was wearing, bright orange bustier with black stockings and a pair of the fuck me pumps. She was working. Kylie paused for a moment, Melissa motioned her over and she slid down next to her. Melissa was totally hot in one of her work outfits. Kylie had a sneaking feeling she was going to be part of a paid show but was a little reluctant. She saw another guy on the video screen this time he had a woman with him. They were naked and chatting with Melissa.

"Girl just come over here and stand by me. Your head will be out of camera."

Kylie stood frozen for a moment.

"It's okay come on just stand here no one will see who you are. You will just be another random tranny cock."

Melissa looked up at her and her eyes went wide with an urgent please etched in them. She looked around the apartment and recalled Melissa had recently lost her job. She must have sold most of her stuff to make rent. Kylie stepped over and handed her a drink.

Melissa started running her hands up and down her legs. The couple could see her body as Melissa started to pull her dress up higher and higher revealing her panties. Kylie watching the reaction of the couple started to get aroused. She drank more of the strong drink and felt the warmth of the alcohol loosen her inhibitions. She helped Melissa arouse her clients. Soon Melissa was giving Kylie head. Kylie was leaned back against the wall as Melissa engulfed her fully over and over again. Kylie closed her eyes and let herself melt into the pleasure. It was a few minutes and she came. Melissa put on a good show and 200 dollars showed up in her paypal account.

"Hundred for you." she said.

Kylie shook her head. "No it's your show. Can you turn that stuff off now I don't want them to see that happens next?"

"Sure baby."

Melissa shutdown the and signed off as Kylie picked an outfit from Melissa's wardrobe. Soon her and Melissa were in each others arms making love in her studio. It was delicate and passionate as you would expect from two sexually active girls.

They made love until almost four in the morning each giving and receiving of each other until they both finally climaxed together during mutual masturbation. It was sexy, fulfilling and as beautiful as any person's healthy sex life.

Young and firm bodies molded by cross-sex hormones pressed together. They understood one another. Each kink and quirk was addressed, with the barrier of acceptance and the awkwardness of gender removed from their interactions they were able to fully explore each other sexually.

Kylie relished the opportunity to give herself to someone fully, as was Melissa. Melissa was quite experienced and smoothly guided Kylie through numerous experiences and heights of ecstasy. Time faded and became non-existent. Only the waves of pleasure washing over her and the tactile adventure of exploring a body not unlike her own. It felt similar but different with each positions change, toy or game they played her sexual boundaries melted into a pool of lube on the satin sheets.

When they were spent. Laying quiet for the next erections to begin, they curled together on the gaudy bed in each others arms and fell asleep.

Five and Six

"So you went home with her.", I said.

"I did."

"And you didn't hit it off?"

"Oh we did, as friends, with benefits. Seems once we got alone at her place we talked for a few hours, drank and fooled around until we passed out. Next morning though, we both admitted we seemed more like girlfriends than lovers. So we decided to keep our relationship there, and now she is one of my best friends, we hookup now and then."

My imagination was running a bit wild with the openness of her sexuality and the potential. But there was so much more to her. As I watched her tell the stories there was a deep level of intellect in her. She was a vastly complicated person and that fascinated me to no end.

"So it seems that so far you have had pretty typical experiences. I mean nothing that is not uncommon for even straight people. Except for the gay stuff anyway."

"Right. Except for the gay stuff." She said shaking her head.

"So you know I am not gay. Did I say that already?"

"Does being with me make you feel gay?"

"I don't know. How do I know what being gay feels like?" I said.

"Well I guess that is a valid observation. How would you know?"

She looked around the park. There was a young man running down the path a few yards down the hill.

"What do you see there?" She nodded to the path.

"A guy running," I said.

"So you don't see a *hot* guy running there?"

"Nope. Not hot. Just a guy."

"Well if you had thought *hot* then maybe that would be a gay feeling."

"I see. So that *hot* girl over there with her boyfriend over, what does that tell you?" I pointed at the bus stop behind us. She turned and saw our reflection in the glass shelter. She turned and looked around and was about to say something when our eyes met in the reflection on the bus shelter. She smiled.

"Okay, I get it, clever. You see yourself as my boyfriend then?" she said.

I paused a bit. Watching her in the reflection I could see us sitting here a year from now.

"Yes. I can see that. You have had a boyfriend before so I think you can tell if I am being genuine."

"I have but I only told you about the one. Jack. There were two others. Jordan and Drake. They were best friends, until I came into their life, something that tries to haunt me every day but I have to let it go. I can always assume there is swirly mass of violence around me, just waiting to leap out."

Her face took on an old despair. I saw in her the years of struggle clearly. Other times I saw sadness on her face but this time it broke through and her eyes twinkled with the collecting tears and her lips trembled ever so slightly. She was damaged and emotionally worn out, fragile. I reached over and took her hand as my other hand rested on her shoulder. Her head bowed and gently pulled her close to me until her head rested on my shoulder and her arms slowly wrapped around my waist.

"Sometimes I am so tired. I just want to give up trying and accept that I may never grow old with someone. Never find that love you can't live without," she said.

"If you will let me, I will try."

I felt her squeeze a little harder. She didn't say anything more as we held each other. I was surprised at how soft and warm she felt. She felt good. Good in a way that is rare for me to feel. Not tactile in a sense but something else, something deeper.

The hold, as I will call it, lasted a couple of minutes. We just stood there as people walked past, lost in our own private world of emotion. I just held her, feeling her anxiety slowly subside. We separated and she walked ahead of me, I followed slowly at first then caught up and gave her my arm. She smiled and looked down and took it.

"Okay, I'm good," she said.

"Me too."

"Well I have a couple more. Since I've gone tis far I might as well continue."

"If you want to. But lets walk a bit longer. I know a nice place we can have cocktail.

"Don't you have to go back to work. It's only like 2:30 or so?"

"I already said I was taking the afternoon. So you have me all to yourself for the rest of the day."

She smiled and held my arm a bit tighter. We strolled up the street several blocks stopping to window shop and watch people. We popped into a pub and took a high top near the large windows. She ordered a glass of wine and I had a stout.

The light coming in the window splashed across her face and lit up the edges of her hair again. I could of swore she was sparkling and I could feel her presence near me. That made me feel an indescribable calm as I have never experienced before. She took a sip of her wine and turned to me.

"Okay. Where did I leave off?

Josh, Eric, Jordan and Drake

"Aren't you going out with that girl?" Drake asked.

"Which girl?"

"You know, that girl introduced me to last Friday? At the bar?"

Jordan finished pumping out the last few reps in his upper body routine. Drake was spotting him as he handled the heavy free weights on the bench press. With a last effort he pushed the bar to the top, he nodded and Drake helped him place it on the rack. Jordan sat up on the bench, sweat pouring down his face and onto his already soaked shirt.

"Yeah no. I'm not seeing her anymore."

"Dude. Why not? She is hot."

"I dunno, just wasn't happening really."

"Oh come on, don't give me that. You were

all over her last Friday. Making out, you couldn't keep your hands of her and she didn't say no. What gives? You were a dick again, weren't you?"

Jordan looked around nervously. "I can't say, not here."

"What is so hush hush?"

"Shhhhh, just stop. I'll tell you later okay?"

"What the fuck could be so bad, Dude we are in a gym. Nobody cares."

"Okay, okay."

Jordan leaned in close and said in a quite voice, "She's a dude."

Drake leaned back and said, "Did you just say 'she's a dude'?"

"Yeah, she has a dick."

"A dick? Her? No fucking way."

"Nope she's a trap. I got trapped."

"Whoa. How did you find out?"

Jordan blushed and looked back and forth and said in a hushed voice, "We were making out in the car out front of her place. And well, she, she got a hard on. I reached over and was

—well I grabbed the damn thing. She jumped back and I was like, WTF, kicked her out of the car and boogied."

"Yeah right. Knowing you, you probably freaked out all over her."

"It, you mean it," Jordan said.

"She's not an it, people aren't 'its'"

"Whatever *it* was *it* wasn't a chick."

Drake just shook his head. He sometimes hated how Jordan could be a total jerk about stuff sometimes. Despite that he was Drake's friend for as long as he could remember, for as long as he could remember Jordan was somewhat of a prick.

"Sometimes I wonder why I still hang around with you."

"Because you know I'm an asshole. Most people have to find out," he said and laid back down on the bench for another series of reps.

"Spot me."

Drake remained silent as Jordan finished off his final set on the bench. Drake was thinking about the girl Jordan introduced him to last week. She was a little shorter than he was, obviously athletic, very pretty and she was funny and bright. He thought she was a keeper for sure, at least for him anyway. Odd thing was, even after finding out about her a few minutes ago, he still felt the same.

Later, Jordan and Drake were in the locker room. Jordan went to the bathroom and left his locker open as Drake was drying off. He recalled Jordan getting called that night. He looked back and seeing that Jordan was gone he quickly found his phone in his jeans, woke it up and entered the code to get into Jordan's phone. He quickly navigated to the recent calls sections and noted a few calls to and from the same number on Friday. He made a mental note of the number and quickly put the phone back.

Jordan came back and finished drying off and started to put on his clothes.

"So what was her name again? Kelly?"

"Kylie. It's name was Kylie."

"Her name."

"Whatever. Let's go get a beer."

***

Drake entered Kylie's name next to the search icon and brought up the number he entered three weeks ago. He had found a picture on his phone that he took of her and Jordan on that Friday date and edited Jordan out leaving Kylie as the photo for the contact in his phone. He sat staring at her picture, debating with himself.

He was sitting on his couch watching a movie and eating a cold piece of pizza, alone in his apartment again. His friend Jordon was with his new girlfriend. Their romance took off in the past week and Jordon hasn't had time or the desire to hang out like they use to. Drake was a little jealous and hurt. Jordon and he hung out a lot together. Drake didn't want to admit it to himself but he missed him. There were a number things about Drake he didn't want to admit to himself.

What the hell. She is really pretty. He thought.

He pushed the contact for Kylie and called the number. It rang a few ties and went to voice mail.

"Hi this is Kylie. It's voice mail you know what to do."

"Uh, Hi, this is Drake, we met a month or so ago, well anyway I wondered if you would like to hangout, go out for dinner or something.

I—ah—am sorry about Jordan. He can be a real asshole sometimes—I'll try back later."

Drake ended the call and sat in silence for a minute. He thought he sound desperate. His phone chimed, a text message arrived.

Are you an asshole like Jordan?

Drake replied, *Not asshole, can I call you?*

The phone chimed again.

Sure.

Drake dialed Kylie's number it rang twice and she answered.

"Hi." she said.

"Hey, this is Drake, we met. Jordan's friend."

"I remember. Why do you want to hangout?" Kylie said tersely.

"Oh well, I guess because I've been thinking about you and well I sorta would like to see you again."

"Hmm—so your friend did tell you he assaulted me in his car?"

"Shit—no he skipped that part."

"Figures. What an asshole and you probably are too I am hanging up—"

"No wait! Wait. I'm not at all like him. Don't judge me based on Jordan he is an asshole and I am done making excuses for him. We haven't been hanging out lately, hear me out—please."

"Go on, I'm listening."

"I thought you were pretty and seemed fun to be around and I don't have anyone in my life and haven't for sometime and I honestly was hoping you would be that anyone."

Kylie thought to herself for a few moments. Why should she date this guy. She let out a long slow breath. He did seem nice, a pleasant sort, nice looking too.

"Well—I kinda knew Jordan was going to be dick. I don't know why I went with him. My sense broke down I guess."

"Yeah, I just thought you deserved better

than the likes of him. I don't normally call his old girlfriends—but you—I thought I would take a chance."

Take a chance. Kylie thought about that and the chances she had taken in her life. She knew all to well you get nowhere in life without taking chances and hearing it come from Drake softened her some.

"Let me think about it. That's the best I can do right now. I'll let you know. I have no reason to trust you and too many to not at this moment."

Drake accepted that answer and said, "Can I text you?"

"If you want—no guarantees I will answer. Your pal is on my shit list and I would rather not take a chance of running into him again."

"Yeah I understand. I wouldn't worry about him, he knows not to pull shit when I am around. But I doubt, I'll see much of him for a while."

"Okay. You can text me for now."

Okay. Thanks—oh and you should know. Jordan told me about you—being trans."

There was a long silence

"He did. What did he say?"

"He told me enough to know."

"—and yet you still called"

"Yes. I did. I know and I don't really care. I think you are beautiful and I would be a fool to not ask you out. Really."

Kylie was silent, lost in thought. At length she determined it wouldn't hurt to let him keep in touch for a while and see what happens.

"Well maybe, text me next week."

"Okay. I will."

They hung up.

Kylie milled about the apartment, obviously feeling some anxiety at having memory of the disastrous date with Jordan. He stared blankly at the wall and her mind rolled back to when she was trapped in his car, fearing the worst.

***

Kylie pulled back away from her date

pushing hard against him. She screamed "No!" more loudly this time and reached for the door handle. Jordan kept coming at her, his strong hand had a tight grip on the back of her neck and the other was controlling her left arm.

"Come on suck my cock, tranny bitch. You love it," he said.

She popped the door open and pushed against it, as she did she raised her leg and kicked him square in the chest with her heel. He recoiled back in pain.

"Get the FUCK OFF me asshole!" Kylie screamed as she fell out of the car onto the curb. Before she had the chance to sit up two guys on the street came to her aid. Jordan seeing them rush to her side sped away from the curb and abruptly turned around the corner.

"Hey are you all right?" one of the men said helping her up.

"I am fine. Thanks, that guy was a real jerk. I had to get out of there."

"You want to call the cops?"

"No, no he is gone. He won't be back."

"Are you sure?"

"Yeah, thanks for your help."

Kylie stood brush dirt off her top. She was shaking slightly and seemed a little disoriented.

"You live in our building, upstairs?" he said.

Kylie looked up at the building then at the guys. She recognized them from a few weeks ago, they were moving in to her building a few floors below.

"Oh yeah, I'm 709. Kylie."

"310, Josh and this is my boyfriend Eric."

"Nice to meet you."

Eric stuck his hand out at her and Kylie put her hand out. Eric's hand appeared small in hers. They shook hands and he was staring at her then looked down at her hand again.

"Girl you got huge hands, are you trans?" Eric said.

"Jesus Eric, you don't just ask people that. I'm sorry he didn't mean that."

"Oh no, it's okay. Yes I am trans," Kylie said rubbing her shoulder. A small hole had torn in the shoulder of her top and she had a small abrasion oozing blood.

"See, I told you she was."

"Oh stop already. Girl, you are hurt." Josh said.

"Oh, yeah it's nothing. Damn, tore my top though."

"Come on in I can clean that for you. It could get infected real easy."

"No, no, it's fine."

"Honey it's okay he is a paramedic, he won't accept no. Any way come up we are dying to meet our neighbors and we have cocktails!" Eric laughed. "Oh honey I was fucking with you I have seen you at the club before. You always sit at the bar by the front glass. I know you sort of, it's all good."

Kylie rolled her eyes and nodded, "Okay. Well in that case. I could use a drink."

She recalled vaguely seeing two guys looking at her then talking to each other at the club the other night. She figured it was them having some debate if she was the same 'tranny' upstairs.

"Honey we are mostly harmless, unless you

don't drink, there is no AA meeting in our place, that's for sure."

Kylie and her new found neighbors went inside their building and took the well worn elevator to the third floor. Eric unlocked the four door locks and they walked in.

"Come on in. Have a seat on the sofa, I'll go get my kit." Josh said.

"What would you like? Beer, vodka, margarita?" Eric said as he started pulling glasses out of the cupboard.

"Oh a vodka seven is good."

"Girl after my own heart, lime?"

Kylie nodded as she sat on the sofa. The boy's apartment was similar in layout to hers. The broad connected living and dining flanked with a small hallway with two bedrooms and a bath. They however had much nicer furniture, plants and artwork.

"I like your place. Cool stuff."

Eric was stirring the drinks and brought them over on a classic cocktail platter, he grinned and winked at Kylie then set it down on the coffee table, and put down cocktail napkins then the drinks.

"Just like at the club, thanks."

"At your service, I'll get some snacks." Eric said with a fake server smile and sashayed into the kitchen.

Josh came out of the back room carrying a large blue bag with a yellow paramedic cross on the outside. He opened the kit and put on some gloves. Kylie rolled up her sleeve over the injury. She hadn't noticed that a line of blood had dried on her arm and she jumped a little and moved so it wouldn't drip on the sofa.

"Oh my!"

"I's okay. It's dried." Josh said.

Josh opened up a package and pulled a gauze pad out it smelled of alcohol, he squirted something from a green bottle and then began to wipe up the blood from her arm. His touch was soft yet deliberate. He quickly cleaned the wound and before Kylie knew otherwise had an oversize bandage tied onto her shoulder.

"There you go. Here is a few extra pads to change the dressing. After today you don't have to cover it. Don't get it wet, unless to wash it, for a few days though if you can help it."

"Thanks. That was really nice."

"Hey, it's okay, we have to stick together you know. We are all on the same team."

Kylie smiled and sipped her drink and winced a little.

"Yow, more mixer please!" she called out.

Josh laughed, "That's Eric. He just wants to get everyone trashed."

Eric returned with some cheeses, grapes a few cured meats and crackers and took seat on the end of the sofa in a manner that afforded him conversation with Kylie and Josh. "How have you like the building so far? We looked all over before we settled on this one. It seemed to have a good vibe," He said.

"It's been pretty low key. People seem pretty busy and normal, lot of young single people, a few young couples and several older folk. No wackos as far as I can tell."

"Well that's good. I had a friend that lived on this block a few years ago and he said it was pretty nice."

"Where do they live now?"

"Oh honey he is dead. He got murdered

outside his building," Eric said with a deadpan expression.

Kylie stared at him and blinked.

"Girl I am fucking with you. He moved to Seattle, new job, he's fine."

Kylie shook her head and took another sip and looked over to Josh.

"Oh he is a fun one."

"I know he is always doing that. Half of what comes out his mouth is shit and the other half is crap," Josh said.

"Hey don't be hatin' on me just because I am sexy."

Eric noticed that Kylie was looking at the objects on the coffee table and she pointed at the box atop and board with rows of holes.

"Ahhhh, I see what you are looking at," Eric said.

Eric took a deck of cards out of a small wooden box sitting atop a cribbage board. "You wouldn't happen to play cribbage?"

"As a matter of fact I have played before. I use to play with my father and grandfather. But since I moved out here I haven't run across anyone that plays.."

"Ohhhh MI GOD yes! Josh she plays!" Eric squealed with delight, and grabbed her arm. "We so have to play. Tell me you will play, say yes, yes, yes."

Kylie looked over at Josh, he was fussing with his med-kit wasn't paying attention. "He won't stop, until you play."

"What the hell. If you want to be beat me that badly, I will play."

Eric grinned wide and started shuffling the cards.

"Honey, can you freshen up the cocktails, this is going to take a few drinks to totally destroy this wanna be."

Josh's phone rang he looked at it and said, "It's Tris."

Eric shuffled the cards once more and pickup half the deck and showed the bottom card showing her a 3. Kylie cut the remaining pile and showed a 9. Eric scooped up the cards, nodded and said "Tell her get his butt over here and meet out new neighbor."

Josh walked into the kitchen with their glasses and freshened their drinks as he talked on the phone.

"Oh, Tristan—He came out a while ago and we adopted him. He was sitting all depressed in the bar one night and of course someone that cute cannot go around all mopey. Fresh meat waiting for the picking. Those bitches at the club would of tore him up. We rescued him, just like you! Josh and Eric's home for wayward queers. But its all good, Josh rescued me and we've been together since. Josh honey! You rescued me baby! Love you!"

"Yes honey, love you too." Josh called from the kitchen as he talked on the phone.

Kylie smiled. Josh and Eric oozed such confidence and joy that it was infectious. After a few minutes she felt perfectly comfortable and safe thanks to their hospitality and compassion. She felt the warmth of a building friendship and it was good to feel that again.

Eric dealt the cards out quickly in a manner that exposed his experience. He frowned as he looked at his cards.

"This is shit. Pure shit I just dealt myself. God."

Kylie smiled, *Just like my Dad,* she thought.

As they mulled over their hands, rearranging cards and mumbling Eric took a breath and spoke.

"So who was the dude in the car?"

Kylie looked at the final card dealt and picked it up. Then discarded two into the crib. Eric dropped one card into the crib. Kylie led with a seven.

"Seven—Oh he was a guy I met a few weeks ago. We went on a few dates. Until tonight when I told him I was trans."

Eric followed laying the 8 of hearts. "15 for 2—So he didn't take that too well I surmise."

Kylie laid the nine of hearts. "24 and a run of three—Yeah no he didn't, he went all creepy on me in like two seconds. Note to self: don't tell guys you are trans while in their car."

Eric dropped a 6 on the pile. "30—True that girl. Good thing you in front of the building. It could have gone very badly anywhere else."

"Go—I know, I'm still rattled some from that."

Eric pegged a point and continued play.

"7—That has to be hard. I mean you look

total girl and I am sure straight boys are all up in your shit."

"17—I know. Sometimes I just don't know what to do. Most of the time I meet a straight guy and was attracted to him it has gone badly. Except once but he admitted he was bi after and had kinda read me." Kylie laid a queen.

"27 for two—Well you got us now to protect you and anytime you need me to beat you at cribbage, I am here for you girl." Eric said playing a queen.

"Go—fucker." Kylie said disgusted.

Eric giggled and pegged a point laying the 4 of clubs on pile, "—and 31 for two"

Kylie laid her last card another queen, "Jesus—10—one for last card—nice playing. I see I am going have to concentrate more."

"Girl it's okay. You are upset. Have some more vodka, it'll make you feel better."

Kylie laughed. She is going to like having these guys for neighbors.

Kylie counted out her cards and took her meager points. They played a few more hands, trading the lead back and forth until Eric destroyed her with a massive hand and crib, he pegged out for the win in the following hand.

"Your puny efforts are no match for the *cribbigator*." Eric said in a robotic Austrian accent.

***

A few weeks passed and Kylie had become fast friends with Eric and Josh. They were frequently sharing meals and movies. Melissa would come over and they would all go downstairs for cocktails at the bar on the corner or pasta at the bistro across the street. Melissa and her had set aside their 'benefits' for the time and focused on simply being good friends. Kylie's life felt happy and content but she was still missing the intimacy of a loving relationship.

She had been getting messages and emails from Drake. He kept bugging her for a date. She kept putting him off for a while until she felt she could trust him. Kylie decided to meet him for lunch finally after receiving a text message with a picture of Drake looking sad.

Dialing him back, he quickly answered the call.

"Hey Kylie. This is a surprise. I was getting use to just texting."

"Drake, well I guess I have let you suffer long enough, let's have lunch together this week. How about Thursday?"

"Hey cool, Thursday would be great. I work downtown so any place over here is awesome."

"That is what I thought. I have a morning meeting downtown and then I am free the rest of the day. How about we meet at the Riverwalk bridge at 4th street, 11:30?"

"Perfect I am just a block away. We can walk down the river there are lots of places. We can pick then." Drake said.

"Okay. It's a date then."

"It is. See you there 11:30. If I get held up at all I'll text you otherwise count on my being there five minutes early."

"Okay see you then. Bye."

"Okay, Bye."

Kylie ended the call and returned to the photo in her messages. He is a good looking guy, she thought and smiled to herself.

Kylie drafted a text to her friend and sometimes lover, Melissa.

I got a date with a boy :D

Melissa was an anomaly in Kylie's love life. When she was down, lonesome or depressed Melissa was there to help cheer her up. They had been close ever since that first night at the club and Melissa had taken it upon herself to be there for Kylie, if she needed her. Her phone pinged.

Is he cute?

Kylie smiled and replied. *Of course.*

Keep me posted. :3

k

Kylie thought that maybe Melissa was the one, she does have strong feelings for her but they are different and not the feelings she is expecting to have for someone. Plus Melissa told her to not get hooked on her. She was flying solo and had no intentions of taking on any relationship baggage. It would be bad for the freedom she enjoys currently.

A date with a boy.

They haven't worked out so well of late she thought.

She walked into the great room of the old apartment. The sun was painting the room with a warm soft tone of evening shortly before it disappeared behind the building across the street. She sat on the sofa and looked out the large old windows. The old thoughts came back. *Why bother, nobody wants you. You are a freak. A girl with a cock.* She shook her head a little and tear came out and spilled down her cheek. She laid over resting her head onto the sofa arm and watched the waning sunlight slide behind the building. *I hope he is nice. I need nice. Somebody to tell me I am beautiful.*

The tears wiped from her cheek easily with the back of her hand as she rose to sitting. She kicked off her shoes and dropped her keys from her pocket onto the coffee table. Slowly she rose to her feet and went to the kitchen and poured herself a glass of white wine from the refrigerator. She scanned the fridge for any food. She knew there wasn't really anything in there tonight but habit is hard to break. She reached to put the wine back but kept the bottle and closed the door.

She wandered across the open apartment to the small hallway and went into her bedroom. The room was spartan and clean. She unbuttoned her blouse, set her wine on the night stand and dropped her skirt and blouse to the floor. She stretched out atop of the bed in her bra and panties. Sipping a bit of wine she propped the pillows up and laid back against them. She drank a glass of wine in a few minutes as she digested the day.

She let her knees fall apart giving her thighs a long loose stretch. Looking down she saw the bulge of her flaccid penis lightly tucked into the crotch of her panties. She reached in and rubbed the front slightly and pulled her penis out and let it rest naturally in her underwear. *Melissa loves that.* She thought. *Will Drake? What if he likes it too much?*

She pulled her panties down and slid them down her legs. There it was. Smaller than it was a few years ago. The hair all shaved away and what remained trimmed to a tight and neat strip. Her breast cleavage created a valley that focused onto her eyes onto it, her penis. She thought of Drake's smile and his soft warm voice. Her penis moved a little. She closed her eyes and thought of him in the bed with her now. Kissing her gently under her ear and down her neck. Running his hand across her breasts. Kylie ran her own hand across her breast, squeezing it gently. Her penis slowly rose from the side as it gained rigidity.

She sat up and reached around behind her and undid her bra and pulled it off of her. After another swallow of wine, she laid on the bed and masturbated with her eyes closed and fell asleep.

***

Kylie woke before midnight feeling chilled. The room was dark but for the glow of the street below. The empty wine bottle and half full glass were still on the night stand. Groggily she pulled herself up and picked up her clothes from the floor and placed them in the dirty clothes hamper and went to the bathroom. She pulled the string and light illuminated the white bathroom. Naked she pulled her tooth brush from the cup and applied a swath of paste and started to brush.

As she did she picked up the toilet seat lid and stood in front of the bowl and thrust her hips forward and released a stream as she brushed. *Too lazy to sit. Bad tranny.* She thought. *Stop saying that. Oh fuck it.*

Finishing in the bathroom she went back into the bedroom and found a chemise hanging behind a robe on the closet door. She slipped it on and then rummaged through her underwear drawer for the matching panties. *Shit. Where are they. Ah.* She found the satin and lace panties that came with the elegant chemise. Pulling them on she ran her hands across the fabric on her buttocks and straightened the underwear. Satisfied she pulled aside the top covers and sheet then climbed into bed.

She lay in bed propped up on her pillows and thumbed through her emails, mostly junk and offers from Victoria's Secret, J Jill and Bare Necessities. She made a mental note to check them out tomorrow before work. She scanned through her twitter and facebook feeds. Same old stuff for the most part. A few trans women posted new selfies and she favorited or liked them. She snapped on the light by the bed and arranged herself in bed showing the just enough to be seductive and took her own picture and tweeted it with a message, *Goodnight sweet people.*

She darkened the phone and turned off the light. Laying on her side she let the day drain from her. As her mind drifted a feeling of warmth passed over her as she thought about Drake and their upcoming date. His smile was on her mind as she fell into sleep, her face loose and innocent as peacefully she dreamed.

Seven

I waited. Waited for the story to continue but by this time her face was showing the signs, not just an everyday disappointment but this was something more. I waited.

She smiled slightly and blinked clear a couple of tears. Her cheek crinkled as she swallowed and I heard the air rush in with an uncertainty that belied her calm. I reached across the table with my palm up and took her hand in mine.

"It's okay. You don't need to continue. I understand."

"No. I am sorry. I haven't talked about Drake like this before and I realize now how much I miss him. Despite it being almost a year now—" Her voice trailed off.

She paused and gathered something from deep in her and continued, "He is gone."

She looked at me with tears filling her eyes again. "He is gone. Not dead but who he was is gone. He has brain damage from a beating. His friend found out we were together and they argued. Then Jordan hit him and he went down, hitting his head on the cement and fractured his skull pretty badly. He is in some hospital, where I cannot see him. I heard he is not really *'there'* anymore. His parents knew we were together but not about me. They found out after Jordan hit him. They wouldn't let me see him or contact them ever again. It sucks. His life ruined because of me."

She wiped the tears away with a napkin and her face hardened as she removed the emotion of her recollection.

I sat stunned. What more could possibly happen her? I felt anger bubble up in side me. Anger that people could hurt her or the ones she loves. I held the anger in check and let my own compassion and feelings for her replace the anger, then I found words.

"I am sorry, but it, it isn't your fault. Our culture is more to blame for that. You know that don't you?"

"Yes. I know but it still is hard to shake feeling responsible. Despite all that we know and how we try to make ourselves accepted. And we—we trans people have made a lot of gains but still there is always going to be a few that refuse to accept us. What's worse is I can deal with being hated but when the person I love is persecuted for being with me, I can't cope with that. It is too much. You know? I can't carry that too."

Her vulnerable face was back, her eyes pleaded with me for understanding. I understood.

"It isn't fair and I don't have any answers other than I would accept what ever fate came to me for the opportunity to experience a deeper connection with someone. To fall and to be in love—would be worth it."

I squeezed her hand a little and she placed her other hand over mine and smiled weakly.

"Are you sure? Don't answer that now."

I nodded and moved my hand up her arm as I pulled closer to her. My hand touched her cheek and she leaned in. I kissed her softly on her lips. A short tender kiss.

"I'm sorry," I said.

"For what?"

"Waiting so long to kiss you."

I sat back down and pushed my drink to the side. She still held my hand as we sat silently together.

"Lets walk."

We left the pub together. Her arm wrapped in mine we strolled down the street in the late afternoon. We approached a crossing, the light was red. We faced each other and I slowly pulled her to me. Her arms wrapped around me and we kissed. A classic brazen lovers kiss on the street as traffic zoomed past. Her lips were warm and soft, her breath was slightly cool in my mouth. I felt her. Not just her lips as we kissed but I felt her soul. I felt as if we had always been together.

***

Her hair fell softly across her cheek as she slept. Watching her sleep I was overwhelmed with desire. I brushed her hair away slowly with my fingers as I did her eyes opened and she smiled.

"I dozed off."

"You did."

My lips lowered to hers and we kissed. Slowly at first but as the seconds passed I felt her intensity build. She pulled the cover off her and kicked it aside pulling me onto her. My chest pressed against her breasts as we kissed. Her hands ran through my hair and she gripped my shoulders. I felt pressure on my shoulder. I responded by scooping her up and rolling over. She straddled me. Her long hair hung down and she flipped it back to one side. Her palms pressed on my chest. There she sat grinning. My eyes scanned down her. She was incredibly sexy with her firm breasts and tight abdomen framed by taught muscles. A sparkle winked from her belly ring that shown just over the top of her penis. I reached for it and she moaned slightly as my hand wrapped around her firm cock. She then bent to kiss me again.

We made love again and fell asleep in each other's arms.

***

I guess I am number seven and hopefully the last of her disclosure stories. Life has ways of surprising you. Kylie surprised me. Not because of where she came from and who she was but because of who she is right now. That is all that matters to me. I am falling in love with her, crazy in love and it is wonderful.

Steven I am transgender.

The words that changed my life. She gave me an intimate window into her life and showed me that she is who she is, a woman with all the hopes and dreams as anyone. A woman who is just as deserving of love and compassion as any.

Where we will ultimately end up is yet to be seen but I see her with me, for as along as she will have me.

Printed in Great Britain
by Amazon.co.uk, Ltd.,
Marston Gate.